the wager

By Bill Myers

The Face of God

Blood of Heaven

Threshold

Fire of Heaven

Eli

When the Last Leaf Falls

The Bloodstone Chronicles (children's fantasy series)

McGee and Me (children's book/video series)

The Incredible Worlds of Wally McDoogle (children's comedy series)

Blood Hounds Inc. (children's mystery series)

Secret Agent Dingledorf and his trusty dog, SPLAT
(children's comedy series)

Faith Encounter (teen devotional)

Forbidden Doors (teen series)

SATAN
Too bad it's impossible for anybody to live the
Sermon on the Mount these days.

GOD
What are you talking about? Anybody can live it.

SATAN
Really? Wanna bet?

the Wager

BILL MYERS

ZONDERVAN™

GRAND RAPIDS, MICHIGAN 49530 USA

The Wager
Copyright © 2003 by Bill Myers

Requests for information should be addressed to:
Zondervan, *Grand Rapids, Michigan 49530*

Library of Congress Cataloging-in-Publication Data

Myers, Bill, 1953–
    The wager / Bill Myers.
        p. cm.
    ISBN 0-310-24873-6
    I. Title.
    PS3563.Y36W34 2003
    813'.54—dc22   2003014644

Published in association with the literary agency of Alive Communications, Inc., 7680 Goddard Street, Suite 200, Colorado Springs, CO 80920.

Interior design by Beth Shagene

Printed in the United States of America

03 04 05 06 07 08 09 /❖ DC/ 10 9 8 7 6 5 4 3 2 1

For Michael Katzenberger: Pursuer of God

Author's Note

This little adventure is a bit different from my others. I wanted to write something that was as much a Bible study as it was a story. If you try reading this as regular fiction, you'll probably be disappointed. Instead of spinning a conventional yarn, I've tried to explore each of the topics in the Sermon on the Mount (in the order they were given) and develop a story around them. By conventional storytelling standards, that is a suicidal approach. But as a means to study Scripture, I'm hoping it will provide some fresh and provocative insights.

At the back, you'll find a Bible study asking questions from each chapter that should help explore these insights a bit more deeply.

Many folks consider the Sermon on the Mount to be one of the greatest single teachings of all time. If this little approach brings any of its truths closer to home, then it has succeeded. And, just so you know, we've stacked the deck a bit with a handful of folks who are praying that it will touch, encourage, challenge, and minister to you as you read it.

Hope it works. Thanks for taking the journey with me.

Best of blessings,

Bill

www.billmyers.com

the wager

Prologue

FADE IN:

INT. HEAVEN—DAY
The Accuser of the Brethren and his Creator are
having another debriefing. The CAMERA gently moves
in, bringing them into a MEDIUM TWO SHOT.

> GOD
> So, where have you come from?

> SATAN
> You're God. You already know.

> GOD
> Humor Me.

> SATAN
> [reluctantly quoting]
> "From going to and fro in the earth,
> and from walking up and down in it."

> GOD
> You do that very well.

> SATAN
> I've had lots of practice.

> GOD
> And what did you find?

                    SATAN
Things aren't so good.

                    GOD
How so?

                    SATAN
I don't know. The sport is all gone.

                    GOD
"Sport?"

                    SATAN
Everything's too easy. In this
postmodern, whatever-they're-calling-
it culture, there's nothing for me to
do anymore.

                    GOD
You seem pretty busy with the whole
Middle East thing.

                    SATAN
Same ol' same ol'. What I mean is,
there's nothing I can sink my teeth
into. Your boys are barely offering
resistance.

                    GOD
For now. But keep your eyes open.

                    SATAN
What? You're going to pull that whole
darkest before the dawn routine again?

                    GOD
Could be.

                    SATAN
You're so predictable.

                    GOD
It always seems to fly.

                    SATAN
But where are Your saints who struggle

with purity? I mean, if nobody's
buying into holiness these days, who's
left for me to accuse and torment for
failing?

                    GOD
I've still got a few out there.

                    SATAN
          [sighing in exasperation]
It's not like the good old days. The
only time holiness comes up is when I
make a joke about it in the sitcoms
and movies.

                    GOD
Talk about being predictable.

                    SATAN
It always seems to fly. Seriously, do
you remember way back when people
actually tried to live the Sermon on
the Mount?

                    GOD
          [smiling in memory]
Yes.

                    SATAN
Now most treat it like some hyperbole,
like an impossible theory that can't
be lived.

                    GOD
Shouldn't that make you happy?

                    SATAN
Like I said, the challenge is gone.
Nobody's even trying to live by those
standards. Nobody can.

                    GOD
Actually, that's not true. Anybody
can.

                    SATAN
Yeah, right.

                     GOD
I'm serious.

                    SATAN
Anybody?

                     GOD
Certainly.

               [Satan scoffs.]

                     GOD
I'll prove it. Pick anybody you want,
anybody at all, and I'll prove to you
that they can live the Sermon.

                    SATAN
          [rubbing chin with claw]
Anybody?

                     GOD
How 'bout that prostitute you're
tormenting with AIDS on Beeker Street?

                    SATAN
Nah.

                     GOD
Okay. Then the abused orphan you're
starving to death in Kinshasa?

                    SATAN
Way too easy.

                     GOD
How's that?

                    SATAN
They've got nothing to lose.

                     GOD
All right, then—you pick one.

                    -14-

                    SATAN
Let me see. The Academy Awards are
coming up in a couple weeks, right?

                    GOD
Right.

                    SATAN
Isn't one of Your boys up for Best
Actor?

                    GOD
               [warmly]
Michael Steel, yes. A good man, though
carrying a lot of excess baggage.

                    SATAN
          [more chin rubbing]
Then I want him.

                    GOD
What? You're not serious?

                    SATAN
Yes, very serious.

                    GOD
I'll need time to prepare him.

                    SATAN
Don't give me that. You're omniscient;
You've known this conversation was
going to happen since the beginning of
time.

                    GOD
Good point.

                    SATAN
So, what do You say? Do we have a
deal?

                    GOD
You sure you want Michael? The poor
fellow has so much on his plate right
now that—

SATAN
I want Michael Steel.

GOD
Yes, but his sister is soon going to—

SATAN
I want Michael Steel.

[Pause.]

GOD
You're getting better at this, you
know.

SATAN
So, do we have a deal?

GOD
The usual emissaries?

SATAN
But not a lot of miracles. I hate it
when You—

GOD
He's My son.

SATAN
I can appreciate that, but—

GOD
[firmly]
He's My son. I'll be there when He
needs Me.

SATAN
All right, all right. But we have to
set a time limit. None of this
deathbed repentance stuff.

GOD
What do you have in mind?

SATAN
Before the Academy Awards.

                    GOD
That's ten days away. Don't be
ridiculous.

                   SATAN
You're also omnipotent, remember.

                    GOD
You are getting better at this.

                   SATAN
He'll have to fulfill all the terms of
the Sermon on the Mount before the end
of the Academy Awards. So do we have
ourselves a bargain?

                    GOD
          [slowly, thoughtfully]
Yes ... we have ourselves a bargain.

                              FADE OUT

I awoke, my heart pounding. I rolled onto my back and took a deep breath. Before I could stop myself, I reached over for Tanya, my wife of twenty years. But, of course, she wasn't there. She hadn't been there in months ... years, if you count her emotional departure. But I still reached for her—sometimes when I was half-awake like now, other times in my sleep, waking up with nothing but her pillow in my arms. Wishful thinking? I suppose. Or maybe a type of prayer. It didn't matter. She was never there. Only the empty spot in our bed where she had once slept ... and the hollow void in my chest where she had once lived.

I opened my eyes and stared up at the ornately carved walnut ceiling. No need to check the clock. The time didn't matter. I wouldn't be able to go back to sleep. Not now. I hadn't been able to after the first dream, and there was no way I could after this one. It was so vivid, so real.

With another breath, this time for resolve, I pulled back the covers and threw my feet over the edge of the bed. I rose, my left ankle stiff and burning—a reminder of the fencing stunt gone bad nearly a year ago. It also served as a testimony of my increasing age and my reluctant acceptance of the studio's demand that I now have a stand-in double, no matter how simple the stunt.

Old age stinks, even at forty-five.

I hobbled into the bathroom and snapped on the lights (enough to illuminate a small city). In the multiple mirrors stood the half-naked body that last year's *People* magazine had named "One of the Ten Sexiest Men in America."

I snorted in disgust. If they only knew what he was like on the inside.

And outside? The outside was nothing money couldn't buy . . . as long as you didn't mind spending three hours a day with a personal trainer, having every scrap of food examined and approved, and, as embarrassing as it is to admit, allowing yourself to be talked into having the excess luggage around your eyes removed.

I turned and leaned closer to one of the mirrors. No amount of money could remove the faint white scars that ran across my shoulders from an overzealous preacher father who looked for every opportunity *not* to spare the rod. Scars that my shrink insists go much deeper. But those scars are insignificant compared to the ones my sister will forever bear from that monster.

I glanced at the Rolex on the marble counter.

4:10.

In an hour the studio driver would pick me up and take me to the set of *The Devil's Breath*, third in the series of Chad Slayter, NSA pictures. The series was your typical mindless, big-budget carnival ride. But it kept my agent happy by thrusting me into the spotlight and the studios happy by making tons of cash. And me? Of course I liked the fame and money; who wouldn't? But I was also grateful for the financial opportunity it gave me to sneak off to do little pictures that actually involved more acting than car chases. And it was one of those little pictures that had thrown me into this year's Oscar hopper.

Did I deserve the nomination? Of course not. Still, it was a nice gesture. Apparently the idea of not forgetting my starving-artist roots and doing a little project had pushed the right political buttons.

But for me the nomination was much more than that.

It was this nomination (along with Tanya's frequent railings at my hypocrisy) that had driven me to try and be a better Christian. Why? Because I was trying to earn Cosmic Brownie Points to win the Award? Hardly. In fact, it was just the opposite. No matter what anybody says, there's nothing that challenges a person's faith like success. What do the Scriptures say? *"A man is tested according to the praise given him."* It's true. The nomination only brought to a head the diseases that had been festering inside my soul for years. Now, more than ever, people were treating me like royalty, offering me all manner of kingly pleasures—every indulgence you can imagine, and some you don't want to. And, at least for me, at least for someone who claims to be a follower of Christ, things had gotten very dangerous.

So I did what any halfway serious person of faith would do when temptation threatens. I hunkered down and tried to follow God more closely—reading my Bible, praying, going to church, being on my best behavior.

Then, exactly one week ago tonight, I'd had the first dream. Except for one element, it had been nearly identical to tonight's. Nearly identical and just as unnerving. It had been so clear and vivid that when I awoke I grabbed my Bible, crossed to my leather reading chair near the fireplace, and began studying the Sermon on the Mount. I read it once, twice, and then, just as the Santa Monica mountains began glowing with a sunrise, I closed the book and said a prayer. Right then and there I had made a promise to God Almighty that I would try to live by these exacting standards. After all, if Christ had spoken the words, and if I claimed to be a Christian, the least I could do was live them.

Unfortunately, I soon discovered that the vow was a lot easier to make than to live. Within hours I was messing up again. And, gradually, as the days passed, I let the promise slip into the well of good intentions. I figured God understood. After all, the Sermon was a worthy principle to strive for, but certainly not something you could live on a daily basis. That was the unspoken understanding I thought we had reached.

Until tonight.

Until the dream returned.

I said it was *nearly* identical to last week's—just as real, just as unnervingly vivid—except for the addition of one important element. In tonight's encounter the two had finally reached their conclusion. God and the Devil had finally selected their participant.

Tonight, they had both agreed that it would be me.

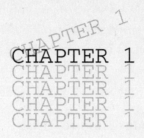

CHAPTER 1

"Now when he saw the crowds, he went up on a mountainside and sat down. His disciples came to him—"

I stared at the radio in disbelief. Not only had I been dreaming about the Sermon on the Mount, but now some preacher was reading and ranting about it over the car radio. How strange. And how sad. Because the more I heard the words, the heavier they weighed on me . . . and the more hopeless I became. That's why I'd borrowed my producer's Lexus and was heading east on Hollywood Boulevard to visit my sister. We were filming less than a mile away and had taken a short break. What better time to swing by and see my Annie, a fellow prisoner of the past. My Annie, a tent peg in the fiercest storms.

"And he began to teach them, saying: Blessed are the poor in spirit, for they-ers is the kingdom of heaven."

His speech, craggy, breathless with old age, and drawling, betrayed his Southern roots—which accounted for the occasional extra syllable. I'd grown up with these words. Heard them all my life. But, as I had climbed the entertainment ladder, the principles had begun slipping through my fingers like water. How could I be *poor in spirit* when every move in my business is calculated to scream, *"Look at me! Pay attention to me! Come see the movie because of me!"* And if *I'm* not screaming them, then I'm paying big bucks for my publicist or my agent or my manager to scream them.

Of course, I'm not foolish enough to believe my own press. I know Michael T. Steel is simply a commodity, something that has to be sold and marketed like dishwashing soap. Yet no matter how hard I try, some small part of me still buys into what is being sold. Those are the times I want to shower, to try to scrub off the pride that keeps seeping up through my pores. But it doesn't work. Because, like the hypocrisy of the scribes and Pharisees, a little leaven really does leaven the whole loaf.

I approached Mann's Chinese Theater and turned left onto Sycamore where a handful of dilapidated homes from the twenties and thirties still stood. Halfway up the block I pulled into an empty space. All this as the preacher continued:

"Blessed are those who mou-wern, for they will be comforted."

I snorted in self-contempt, then slipped on some Elvis sunglasses and a moth-eaten stocking cap, courtesy of the Wardrobe Department. (The last thing I wanted right now was to be recognized.) I threw a glance at the parking meter, grateful for the time still on it, then shook my head with more disgust. What did I care about parking money? With a current deal of twenty million dollars, against fifteen percent of gross, what did I care about the cost of anything? I had more money than I could spend in a lifetime. In two lifetimes. *Mourn?* What did I have to mourn about?

Unfortunately, nothing.

"Blessed are the meek, for they will inherit the earth."

He just kept piling it on, didn't he? *Meek?* Anything I knew about meekness was long forgotten—replaced by demands for bigger dressing rooms, more screen time, my name above the title. *Meekness?* There was no meekness in my life. I closed my eyes and rested my forehead on the leather steering wheel. I had everything and then some. And now I had the audacity to feel terrible about it? Or—let's be honest here—to feel terrible for not feeling terrible about it? How sick is that?

But that's why I was here.

I didn't come often. Schedules and my rise in popularity made that close to impossible. But this afternoon, since we were shooting a second-unit car chase on La Brea, and since Wardrobe let me sneak off with the clothes I'd been assigned—well, here I was ... once again trying to find some sort of "center."

"Blessed are those who hunger and thirst for righteousness, for they will be filled."

I lifted my head from the steering wheel with a rueful smile. I finally got one right. At least I was hungry. Still, I doubted one out of four was exactly the percentage Christ had in mind when He gave the Sermon. I turned off the ignition and climbed out of the car. Pulling the trench coat from the backseat, I slipped it on over my raveling sweater and stained wool pants. I shut the door, beeped the locks, and started forward.

Heat and blinding light reflected off the sidewalk. It was midafternoon and well into the eighties. Thanks to the heavy clothes, I felt every degree.

Up ahead stood a two-story white house with green shutters. "Jeremiah's Place." It was a halfway house where the dregs of society stayed until they were strong enough to reenter life ... or sink back into the dregs. Runaways (boys and girls), pimps, druggies, hookers (boys and girls), street crazies—anyone who had fallen through the cracks or had been swept under society's rug. These were the people my Annie worked with day in and day out.

I noticed activity on the front porch. Some white chick was cowering behind a big black bald guy while a scrawny white kid with dreadlocks was shouting at her.

"You c'mon, now!" the kid cried. "You can't hide here forever! C'mon!"

The girl stayed behind the bald guy who silently held his ground.

"C'mon now, Heather. Don't be makin' it no worse than it is."

It could have been any one of a dozen scenarios. My guess was that some drugged-out hooker was trying to go straight, and her wannabe pimp/boyfriend had come after her. However it fell, the big bald guy (no doubt a staff member) was the only thing between her and bodily harm.

"Girl, I'm not tellin' you again!"

I turned onto the broken sidewalk and headed toward the porch. All three saw me and came to a stop. Big Bald shifted slightly, preparing to hold us both off if he had to.

Now, no matter who you are or how hard you try, there's a certain arrogance that comes with money and power. Let no one tell you different. It may be disguised, but it's always there. And when money and power no longer mean anything, then that arrogance can turn into a type of recklessness, even self-destruction. I suppose that's some of the mode I was operating in now.

"What's going on?" I called.

"This ain't your concern, old-timer," Dreadlocks replied. (I could have done without the handle, but to these youngsters, forty was close to Medicare.)

I started up the stairs slowly, deliberately, taking one step after another.

"Who are you?" Big Bald asked quietly. "What do you want?"

I finished the steps and joined them as Dreadlocks gave another warning. "Be careful, old man."

I raised my eyes to meet his. I could see they were bloodshot from booze or dope or both. This was either going to be a very brilliant move on my part or a very stupid one. Either way, I wanted to enter the house, and the girl obviously needed help. So . . . slowly, I reached for my sunglasses and removed them. Holding his gaze, I quietly folded them and slipped them into my pocket. A spark of recognition flitted across his watery eyes.

Good.

Carefully, and with more than a little drama, I reached up and removed my stocking cap. Never taking my eyes from his, I began folding it.

The spark of recognition flared to a flame. His mouth dropped open. "You're . . ." His voice caught and he lowered it. "You're *him!*"

For a moment I wasn't sure which *him* he was referring to. He looked like a bright kid, but there was all that dope and booze running through him, so it was hard to tell. Fortunately, he didn't keep me in the dark.

"Chad Slayter," he gasped. "NSA!"

Now I knew which card to play. I gave a slight nod and raised a finger to my lips.

"What are you doing here?" he whispered.

I glanced around.

"You on assignment?"

I looked coolly into the eyes.

Raising his hands, he apologized. "I know, I know, man—if you tell me, you gotta kill me—sorry."

Not only was he living in the wrong reality, he was quoting some of its worst dialogue. I looked at him and slowly nodded. Then I motioned to the girl. "She's with me."

Dreadlocks turned to her, his mouth sagging further.

She stared at me and blinked.

"You mean . . . ," he swallowed, then continued, hoarsely, "she works with you?"

"Undercover. Yes."

He looked from her to me and back to her again. Then, breaking into a grin, which broke into a hacking cough he said, "I knew it, girl. I knew there was somethin' different about you."

She continued to stare.

"I knew it," he kept coughing, "I just knew it . . ."

I glanced at Big Bald. His face was street-poker neutral.

". . . I knew you was different."

Turning to Dreadlocks, I asked, "Is that a problem?"

"No man, no problem. Heather here, she was just, you know, hanging with me some, and I thought, you know, she was trying to get smart or somethin', but now I see."

"That's right," I said. "It was all part of her cover."

"Yeah, man, I see, I see. I get what's comin' down."

"We can be assured of your silence?"

"You bet, man. Anything for my country and Chad Slayter. Anything, just name it."

"Good. Then, if you don't mind . . ." I motioned for the girl to join me. She hesitated, until Big Bald nodded permission. I continued. "We have much to do."

"It's cool, man, it's cool. I understand, it's cool."

The girl tentatively approached. I placed my hand against the small of her back and directed her toward the door.

"Hey, wait a minute! Wait a minute!"

I felt her tense. I tried not to as I slowly turned back to him.

"Look, if there's like anything I can do to help, you know. I mean if you need a man on the street, like to watch your back, just say the word. 'Cause when it comes to the street, I know all and see all, you know what I mean? Just say the word and I'm there."

I looked him over then gave the slightest nod—part agreement, part dismissal—before turning and heading for the door.

"You take care, Heather," he called after us. "You keep doin' us proud, you hear?"

Big Bald stepped ahead of us and opened the door. As we passed, his eyes caught mine and he quietly whispered, "It's good to see you, Mr. Steel. Your sister's inside."

— — —

"I swear, Toad, you are some piece of work." Annie gave one of those laughs of hers—part mocking, part good-natured ribbing. A laugh that, even as kids hiding in the basement from our father, gave some comfort and assurance of greater wisdom. "Don't you get it?" she asked.

"Get what?"

"You *already* qualify!"

I frowned as we made our way out of the kitchen, drinking caffeine-free Diet Cokes. We walked through the living room and headed for the stairway. I slowed and waited patiently as she limped up the creaking stairs ahead of me, as she grabbed the banister and pulled herself up one step after another. I'd learned years ago never to offer help.

As we continued, I looked about the house. It hadn't changed much—same old musty smell, same wooden floors, same donated furniture. Most of the staff and residents were new, but even they held a familiar look of wornness.

An older man, in his sixties, was on his hands and knees beside an electrical outlet. He muttered to himself as he stuffed tightly folded paper into each hole of the receptacle.

"How's it going, Bill?" Annie asked.

"Just couple more to do, Miss Annie," he answered without looking up. "Then no more electricity leaking out on the floor."

"And no more aliens drinking it up at night?" she asked.

"One can only pray, Miss Annie. One can only pray."

"Amen to that," she said. We continued up the stairs as he resumed his muttering and folding of paper.

I quietly smiled and thought, as I occasionally did, how the two of us used our pasts (or how they used us) in choosing our professions. Annie, with her firsthand experience of abuse and suffering, was able to reach out to others who suffered . . . while receiving from them the heartfelt love that she so desperately needed. And me? I suppose I had the same need to be loved, I'd just found a different way of earning it.

We reached the top of the stairs, turned right, and headed down the hall to her office—a tiny sweatbox of filing cabinets, sagging shelves, thumbtacked pictures on the wall, overflowing bulletin boards, and a roaring window fan. I'd frequently offered to donate central AC to the ministry's house (as well as a new house) but Annie always turned me down, insisting that the church and community needed to support them. Something about taking ownership and building relationships. I didn't fully understand it then or now, but I knew better than to argue. Once Annie made up her mind, trying to change it was a waste of time.

She'd barely kicked off her shoes and plopped behind the old steel desk before I got back on topic. "What do you mean, 'I qualify'?"

"I mean, the very stuff you're talking about . . . *"poor in spirit, meek, mourning, hungry for righteousness"* . . . the fact that you feel so awful about not having them means that you're already *poor in spirit*, and *meek*, and *mourning*, and *hungry*."

I closed my eyes and tried again. "You don't understand what I'm saying."

"I understand perfectly. I understand that you're going through another one of your little self-analytical actor things."

"How can you say that?"

"'Cause it's true. There's no one harder on Toad than Toad. And now that you're a big shot, up for the Oscar in what, two weeks?"

"Ten days."

"Ten days—you're going to be even tougher on yourself."

"Shouldn't I be?"

"Of course you should. You of all people."

I scowled.

"Look." She ran her hand through the tight curls of her auburn hair. "I got religious supporters coming through here every other day—arms folded in smug piety, confident of their faith, as they busily write checks for us."

"And you're not grateful?"

"I'm ecstatic. That's not the point. The point is, they think they've got it all together. They're not hungry for God anymore. But you, little brother, your arms are reaching out, begging for help."

"Because I need it."

"And that's why you're blessed: You *know* you need it. The same goes for those who are poor and meek and mourn and hungry—they know they need God."

I shook my head, still not entirely buying it.

"Let me ask you. If you were God, whose hands would you fill—someone who's got them stuffed piously in their pockets? Or someone who's got them wide open and pleading for help?"

"But—"

"Annie?"

We looked to see a staff member at the door. She was a gaunt bottle-blonde, obviously an alumnus from the street.

"It's Mrs. Clouda again."

Annie nodded and blew a tendril of curls out of her eyes. She motioned for me to hold my thought as she reached for the phone. "Hello, Mrs. Clouda."

She listened patiently then rolled her eyes at me. The woman was obviously giving her an earful. Covering the mouthpiece, she whispered, "She turned eighty-seven last week. Want another Diet Coke?"

I shook my head.

She spoke back to the phone. "I appreciate your frustration, Mrs. Clouda, but—"

More listening.

"Yes . . . yes . . . but I have to call the paramedics every time you attempt suicide. It's the law."

I raised an eyebrow.

She shook her head and hit the mute button, still keeping the receiver to her ear but free to talk. "She calls in a couple times a week. Me and the boys at the fire station are her only social outlet. Now, where were we?"

It took a moment to gather my thoughts. "It's just—I've been having these dreams that God is pretty serious about the Sermon on the Mount and—"

"Of course He is."

"Right. But how can I—"

She hit the mute button and spoke. "From New Jersey, you say. Do they ever come out and visit you? Uh-huh . . . uh-huh . . . I see . . ." She pressed the mute button and looked at me, waiting for more.

"I don't know," I sighed. "Maybe I should just chuck it all and come here to work with you."

"Right, quit the hard life and find something easy to do." She gave me her famous lopsided grin.

"You know what I mean," I insisted.

She pressed the mute button. "So the paramedics are there now? Yes, Mrs. Clouda, it would be a fine idea if you let them in. Yes, dear, I can wait." Hitting the mute button she looked back to me. "Listen, Toad, we all have our wars. And changing from one battlefront to another doesn't make them any easier."

"Yes, but, at least—"

"Besides, you'd just be coming here for a religious high."

"Pardon me?"

"The thrill of self-sacrifice. The joys of martyrdom." She shook her head. "No way, little brother. That stuff never lasts."

Before I could argue, she was back on the phone. "Hey, Brad, Annie from Jeremiah's Place. Everything okay?" She paused a moment then nodded. "Great. No, go ahead and put her back on. Catch you later." She turned to me, waiting.

"You don't think I could last here?" I asked, using all of my acting skills to avoid sounding defensive.

"Not a week." Then, shrugging, she added. "Someday, maybe, when you're ready. But not now, no way."

"What's that supposed to mean, 'When I'm ready'?"

She shook her head. "You've got it made in the shade, pal. Movie star, beautiful wife, fancy homes, loved by millions."

"But it doesn't mean anything!"

She nailed me with a look that was more than skeptical.

I tried to explain. "Here, I mean at this house, you're really touching people, you're really being an influence."

"And you're not? The fact that millions of people watch you, that they want to be just like you—you don't think that's touching people, being an influence?"

I sighed wearily. "But what kind of influence?"

"I guess that's up to you." She returned to the phone. "Right here, Mrs. Clouda. Yes, they are nice boys, but you can't have me calling them for no reason." She paused a moment. "Yes, they said you had the gas on full—but they also said you didn't bother to blow out the flames." Another pause. "No, I appreciate a woman your age can't remember everything, but—"

I shook my head, musing at the scene as they shared more chitchat until it finally drew to an end.

"Okay, dear. Thanks for calling. Yes, I think the world of you too. Bye-bye." She took a deep breath and hung up, blowing more hair from her eyes.

"Two times a week?" I asked.

She nodded.

"Are there others like her out there?"

"Enough." Then, focusing her attention back on me, she said, "Listen, if you really want to do some guilt relief and get your hands dirty, I've got a project you might be interested in."

"Yeah?"

She leaned past me and called out the door. "Charlie?"

No answer.

"Charlie, I know you're there. Charlie, will you come in here, please?" She lowered her voice. "He's been sitting in the hallway ever since you came in." Mouthing the words, she added, "Big fan."

I nodded as a skinny nine- or ten-year-old appeared in the doorway. He kept his head lowered, eyes riveted to the floor.

"Charlie, this is my brother, Michael Steel. Michael, this is Charlie."

"Hey, Charlie," I said, smiling.

He continued staring at his shoes.

Annie explained. "Social Services assigned him to us, until they can locate his parents." Turning to him, she added, "But at the moment, you're not giving us any clues, are you, Charlie?"

He gave no response.

"But he sure does love the movies. Fact, I hear someday he plans on being a big star, just like you."

That brought the slightest of nods.

"He's especially fond of Chad Slayter, NSA."

"That so?" I asked.

"In fact, rumor has it that he's got the lines from both of the movies memorized. Isn't that right, Charlie?"

A little shrug.

"No kidding," I said. "That's quite an accomplishment."

More shoe staring.

"Did you know we're filming Part Three?" I asked. "In fact, we're less than a mile from here."

His face shot up to mine in excitement. And what I saw made me gasp.

Annie chuckled softly. "Looks familiar, does he?"

I continued to stare. And for good reason. I was looking into a child's face nearly identical to my own at that age. Same chin, same thick eyebrows, same brown hair spilling over the forehead. And the same liquid dark eyes. But it was more than our physical similarities. There was something else, something deeper. As I looked into those eyes, so full of awe and wonder, I felt an immediate connection. It was like looking back thirty-five years into the soul of another boy. One equally consumed by movies—one equally vulnerable, equally filled with pain and hope.

"You said you were filming nearby?" Annie asked.

I blinked, then swallowed, coming to. "We sure are." I forced what I hoped to be an engaging smile. "In fact—," I glanced at my watch. "Shoot! I need to get going! We've got a beach scene scheduled at 5:00." I quickly rose, but barely made it to my feet before an idea formed. "Annie . . ."

"Yeah."

"If Charlie here is a big fan of Chad Slayter, and if we're filming not too far away at the Santa Monica Pier . . . maybe he could . . . I mean, do you think you could fix things so we could . . . ."

She was grinning mischievously. "It's already done."

CHAPTER 2

CHAPTER 2
CHAPTER 2
CHAPTER 2
CHAPTER 2

"So, you ever see a film shoot before?" I asked Charlie as we climbed into the car. It wasn't a stupid question. Film shoots for Los Angelians are as common as car crashes—and often as inconvenient. Most pause or rubberneck just long enough to see if they can spot a star, then move on, grumbling about the tie-up of traffic.

But Charlie was too taken by my producer's Lexus, with its fancy leather seats, dash gizmos, and high-tech sound system, to give an answer.

I smiled, then remembered something else he might find interesting. "Hey, Charlie," I said, reaching into my pocket. "Check this out." I produced my own set of keys . . . with one very unique addition. "You remember in *Chad Slayter, The Kiss of Death*, the diamond ID that operated his super spy-car?"

Charlie nodded and I held open my hand. His eyes widened like saucers. For there in my palm was the very same clear-plastic ID with the carved initials, C. S., that we'd used as a prop in the movie.

He continued to stare, speechless.

I chuckled quietly. "You can hold it if you want."

He looked to me for confirmation.

"Sure, go ahead."

With great care and reverence he reached out and took the ID into his hands. The sun refracted in the plastic prism, throwing a rainbow across his face that danced and shifted with the moving car. He swallowed, not saying a word, not moving a muscle. Only staring.

I remained silent, stealing occasional glances at him from the road, trying to imagine the awe and wonder he must be feeling. It was then that another idea came to mind. "Listen, if you want, maybe we can get you on the shoot as an extra tonight—you know, as one of the background people on the beach or something."

His eyes shot to mine in astonishment. And, for the second time that afternoon I felt the connection, that transportation back to my own childhood. I didn't pretend to know Charlie's particular ghosts, but it didn't matter. Like me, like the thousands of hopefuls that are drawn to this town every month, I could see that movies and his dream of being a star were his hope for escape. All he had to do was become famous and everyone would love him. After all, acting equals stardom, which equals love. It's a foolish equation but one that attracts us to the profession in droves.

I turned my attention back to the road. Since the 10 Freeway would be jammed (the 10 Freeway is always jammed), I'd taken Sunset to the 405 where we would drive to Santa Monica Boulevard and head straight for the pier. So far, Charlie hadn't said a single word. Which was okay. I didn't push. He'd talk when he was ready.

I pulled out my cell phone and checked messages. They were the usual . . .

2 from my agent, no doubt sweating bullets over my
    disappearance

4 from various assistant directors, sweating the same bullets

1 from a neurotic, wannabe producer trying to put together a
    movie package

1 from Tanya

1 from Robert Meisner, my current producer

As much as I wanted to return Tanya's call, I passed, at least for now. She had a way of ripping out my heart, dropping it on the floor, then walking off and leaving me groveling, trying to put it back inside. I couldn't afford that, not tonight. The scheduled scene could be an emotional drain. I needed to have enough energy to pull it off. Talking to Tanya beforehand would ensure that I wouldn't. I'd call her back when we were done, though. Like some faithful dog who can't help himself, I always called her back.

The other messages could wait, except for Robert's. A producer in the middle of a shoot is like someone running ahead of a freight train . . . but just a little slower. Robert's concerns were always pure and unwavering. First, last, and foremost, they were always for Robert. Still, I figured he had enough worries without fretting about where his star had disappeared to, so I hit his number and waited.

In the silence I glanced back at Charlie. "You can turn on the radio if you want."

He flashed me a crooked-tooth smile and turned on the radio. To my surprise, the same preacher was still on the air. Not only that, but he'd picked up exactly where he'd left off an hour and a half earlier. I shook my head in quiet amazement.

"Blessed are the merciful, for they will be shown mercy. Blessed are the pure in heart, for they will see God. Blessed are the peacemakers, for they will be called sons of God."

"Feel free to find another station," I said.

Gratefully, his hand shot to the selector and he began cruising the dial just as Robert answered the phone with his typical, "What!"

"How's the war?" I asked.

"Michael! Where are you!?"

"Call time isn't 'til 5:00. You loaned me your car to run some errands, remember?"

"It isn't that, it's—"

I heard screaming and swearing in the background. There was a brief rustle of the phone being covered, more muffled oaths, this time Robert's, and then he was back. "Michael, you gotta get over here—now! Cassandra's lost it!"

"Again?"

"This time it's serious. She won't listen to anybody."

"What can I—"

"She trusts you, Mikey. Everybody trusts you."

There was more screaming, more phone rustling, more muffled oaths. A moment later he was back. "Just get here, Michael! Get here as soon as you can!"

– – –

In the parking lot, directly beside the beach, was the production's usual assortment of semis, panel trucks, trailers, and vans. In many ways, big shoots like these remind folks of a carnival or a circus. But instead of three rings, our circus has dozens—with much more drama going on, not only in front of the camera, but behind.

I stole a look at Charlie. He was glued to the window taking it all in.

The guard motioned us past the barricades to another guard who directed us into a space beside my dressing room trailer. I'd barely pulled to a stop before heads turned toward us and people started forward.

"Get ready, Charlie," I said as I reached for the door. "Things may get bumpy."

I stepped out of the car and the onslaught began . . .

"Mr. Steel," a brand-spanking-new assistant director, just slightly older than this morning's paper, scampered toward me. His predecessor had been fired yesterday and this newbie was determined to prove his invaluableness. "We've got to get you into Wardrobe."

"Mr. Steel," another youngster, an assistant dietician, approached. "Chef wishes to know if you would prefer regular or garlic butter upon your croutons."

"No butter!" my trainer, a burly Austrian (is there any other type) appeared beside me.

"But the butter is essential to the crouton's texture and consist—"

"Mr. Steel . . . ," the assistant director pleaded.

"Charlie," I motioned for him to join me. "Stay close."

"And no croutons!"

"Michael!" I looked up and saw Robert Meisner, a short, muscular man, approach. "Thank goodness you're here."

"Fat and carbs, they defeat the entire purpose of the salad!"

"But—"

"And we better be talking Romaine lettuce! Tell me we are talking Romaine!"

"What's wrong?" I asked Robert as he arrived.

"Cassandra. She's gone off the deep end."

I rested my hand on Charlie's shoulder, gently guiding him through the crowd.

"Cute kid," someone from Makeup commented.

"Is it his?" another half-whispered.

Robert continued. "She claims we've violated some clause in her contract."

"Did you?" I asked.

"Of course not!"

I gave him a look.

"How should I know?" Running his hands through his new hair plugs he cried, "She's got so many of them!"

"Mr. Steel. *Please.* Wardrobe is waiting."

I gave a nod and pulled Charlie closer.

"Michael!" Kenneth Halvstein, my agent, stood in the distance, shaking his cell phone at me. "It's looking good, my friend—very, very good." He no doubt meant the Oscar votes. He'd been on the phone doing some last-minute campaigning. Let no one tell you there isn't politics in the Oscars. And rumor had it that this particular election was going to be close.

"What?" My trainer was shouting at the dietician. "You are mixing fruits and vegetables! Have you lost your mind?!"

"Mr. Meisner," a production assistant appeared behind Robert holding a tray of coffee, tea, and sparkling water. It was essential he memorize what we each preferred.

"Not now!" Robert snapped. Carefully guiding me over the ruts in the sand, like I was his elderly grandfather, he explained. "We were in the middle of a crane shot, moving in for a close-up, when she suddenly throws up her hands and runs off the set screaming something about the death of innocent animals!"

"Mr. Steel, would *you* like your coffee now or—"

"Leave us alone!" Robert shouted.

"Gentlemen," the newbie resurfaced to my left. "We've got to get Mr. Steel into Wardrobe immed—"

"Wardrobe?" Robert roared. *"Wardrobe?"*

Not knowing enough to duck and cover, the kid motioned toward the director, Colin Buchanan. "Mr. Buchanan says we need to start rehearsing the scene if we're to stay on schedule—"

"Schedule? *Schedule!*" The veins in Robert's temple bulged. "Without an actress we don't have a schedule! Without an actress we don't have a movie!"

Unsure what to do, the newbie blinked, then swallowed, looking very much like the proverbial deer in headlights.

I glanced at Buchanan sitting in his chair, reading script pages and letting them fall, one after another, to the sand where they proceeded to blow down the beach. Twenty yards behind him, out of his sight, production assistants were scurrying this way and that trying to catch them.

"What's with him?" I asked Robert.

"He's reading the rewrites you asked for."

"Doesn't look too thrilled."

"You think?" Robert asked.

"Are we going to have trouble?"

"One fire at a time, Michael, one fire at a time."

We arrived at Cassandra's dressing room trailer. It was easily twice as large as mine and twice as expensive. Custom-made. From what I'd heard, about $200,000 worth of custom-made. Demanding the biggest and best trailer on a shoot is standard operating procedure for high-maintenance stars who need to prove they're the most important member of the cast. I usually don't play that game. My upmanship is more subtle. When I hear of such maneuverings, I merely tell my agent to kick up my gross percentage another half point. A $200,000 trailer that you only use for sixteen weeks during the shoot, or an extra three quarters of a million dollars? You be the judge.

Robert reached up and knocked ever so tentatively on the mahogany door that read "Cassandra" (she never used her last name) in laser-carved cursive.

"Get away!" came a scream, followed by the crashing of what could only be fine china, or fine crystal, or . . . well, whatever it was, I could see Robert wince. Not at the crash, but at the extra production cost. "Leave me alone!" the voice screamed. "You're murderers! All murderers!"

Robert glanced at me. I took a breath. The last thing I wanted to do was enter this den of insanity. For a moment I nearly changed my mind. This was Robert's problem. He'd gotten himself into it, let him get himself out of it. Besides, since my contract had the standard pay-or-play clause, it would be a major financial advantage for me if the production shut down. I'd still get full payment. As far as I could tell there was not a single plus for my stepping into this minefield.

Except . . . except . . . those haunting words I'd just heard from the Sermon on the Mount. *"Blessed are the merciful," "Blessed are the pure in heart,"* and . . . here it came . . . *"Blessed are the peacemakers."*

Walking into that trailer was the last thing I wanted to do, but if I was serious about trying to live those words, it was the only thing I could do. Not exactly thrilled with the prospect, I reached up and knocked on the door. "Cassie?" I knocked again. "Cassie, it's Michael. Can I come in?"

There was no screaming this time. And, to Robert's relief, no more crashings.

"Cassie, can I come in a minute?"

No response. Nothing. Well, except for a carefully timed sniffle, projected just loud enough to be heard through the door.

I had my answer and reached for the knob . . . just as Charlie reached out and took my free hand. I glanced down. He looked up entreatingly with those incredible, dark eyes. He wanted to come in, there was no doubt about it. I wasn't sure if this was the best idea, but Charlie was a fan. And Cassandra did love fans.

I weighed the thought another moment, then squeezed the boy's hand as I turned the knob and the two of us stepped into her trailer.

– – –

It was pretty much as I'd expected—plush, forest-green carpet, white-washed oak paneling, a chandelier or two, marble bar top with brass (or could it be gold?) fixtures, plenty of overstuffed furniture, an entertainment center complete with a plasma big screen, and, of course, flowers—every day, dozens and dozens of freshly cut flowers, enough to make any funeral home jealous.

Scattered about the room sat her entourage of half a dozen people (the others must be out shopping). Many stars travel with entourages these days. Some are needed and some, like my last co-star's chef for her pet iguana . . . well, I'm not so certain.

"Michael—," Cassandra dashed toward me, her eyes swollen with tears, yet her makeup completely intact. At one time she'd had one of the most photographed bodies in America, like a Greek goddess, proof that Beverly Hills still had the world's finest surgeons. This was our second picture together. Folks seemed to like our chemistry. With her physique and the way folks publicized my faith, more than one tabloid had referred to us as *Beauty and the Priest*. But now she was in her early forties, and, as each year passed, as that perfect body showed more and more wear, she showed more and more insecurity.

We hugged, a bit too familiarly for some tastes, but she did have her entourage to impress, and she was emotionally distraught.

When we separated, I took her hands. "What's wrong, kiddo?"

She tried to speak but could not. Tears filled those perfect, emerald green eyes, then spilled down her perfect, sculptured cheeks. "Oh, Michael," she sobbed. Unable to continue, she turned to cross the room, but her emotions caused her to stagger, and she caught herself at the nearest chair, slumping into it.

Her entourage gasped. Some rose. One of her miniature shih tzus raced to her chair and hopped onto her lap.

I motioned for Charlie to stay back in the shadows and moved to join her. I knelt before her and gently repeated, "What's wrong, Cassie?"

More sniffs as she tried to speak. Her lips trembled, her mouth opened, but the words wouldn't come. She could only shake her head as she absentmindedly stroked the dog.

I was wondering how much longer this preamble would take when, as if for the first time, she noticed Charlie.

"You have a—," she sniffed bravely, pulling herself together. "You have a guest."

"Yes. I hope you don't mind." I glanced over my shoulder. "This is my friend, Charlie."

She gave a brave smile. "Hello, Charlie."

"He's quite a movie buff," I said.

"Are you, now?" she asked, sniffing.

He nodded as color raced to his cheeks.

"In fact, he knows all the lines from our last Chad Slayter movie by heart. Don't you, Charlie?"

Cassandra looked at me in surprise. I nodded that it was true. Breaking into a broader smile, she turned back to him and magnanimously stretched out her arms. He hesitated, then took a half step into the light.

Cassandra practically gasped, "Why . . . he's gorgeous."

Again she motioned for him to join her, and this time he obeyed. When he arrived, she gave him a hug and a lingering kiss on the check. He flashed an embarrassed grin but didn't wipe it off.

Cassandra smiled, pleased at her power. "Who is he again?" she asked.

"Just a friend."

She nodded. Then, suddenly, tears refilled her eyes.

One of her entourage approached, "Oh, baby—"

But she held out her hand, motioning for him to stay, insisting that she was strong enough to handle the pain.

Now, as best as I could tell, we'd covered the formalities, so I took my cue and again asked, "What is it, Cassie? What happened?"

She took a shaky breath for courage, wiped the tear from her cheek, and began. "You know how passionately I love animals."

I nodded. I didn't know all the details, but I knew she was arrested in an anti-fur demonstration a few months back and that she was a strict vegetarian. I also knew of the clause in her will—that when she died, she was to be cremated and her ashes fed in equal amounts to both of her dogs so she would always be a part of them.

She gave another sniff. "And you know my contract clearly stipulates that no animals will be harmed in the making of my movies."

Again I nodded, hoping she'd get to the point as the leg I was kneeling on had started going numb.

"Well, we were on the beach filming and . . . and . . . ," she swallowed, forcing herself to relive the horror. "And when I looked up I saw,"—the words tumbled out in an uncontrollable cry—"one of the gaffers was wearing gloves!" Her body convulsed, but there was more. "*Leather* gloves!"

Wasted by the memory, she began sobbing uncontrollably. I reached out to hold her hands. She let me take them as she struggled helplessly for control, tears falling from her long lashes.

I remained kneeling, feeling her pain; well, feeling something, before I finally spoke. "Sweetheart, you don't want those nice men to get electrocuted, do you?"

"What nice men?" she asked, confused.

"The gaffers. They work with electricity. They need to protect themselves from—"

"We're talking cows, Michael! Cows that have never hurt anyone!" Again her body shuddered and again she broke into sobs. I nodded and looked up, scanning her entourage. To a person each of them was also in tears.

There was a gentle rap on the door. This time, Cassandra was too spent to answer. So, a moment later, Robert appeared. "Cassandra . . . honey, I don't know what—"

But that was as far as he got before her head snapped up and she shouted, "MURDERER!"

With an ego far greater than common sense, Robert stepped into the trailer, obviously determined to solve the problem face to face.

Cassandra leaped to her feet, sending the shih tzu scurrying and yapping.

"SLAUGHTERER OF INNOCENTS!"

I rose to join her, cautioning, "Cassie . . ."

Robert threw his hands into the air. The only thing greater than his ego was his lack of tact. "You really are nuts, aren't you?!"

Cassandra's body trembled in rage. "MONSTER! KILLER!"

"Look, I came here to tell you, if you don't honor your contract—"

I knew what would happen next, just as clearly as if it had been scripted for a movie. Maybe in Cassandra's mind it already was. She lunged at Robert screaming, "MURDERER! KILLER!"

She landed a couple blows against his chest but nothing too dangerous (which, of course, was intentional) as he tried his best to grab her arms. I'd seen the scene in a hundred movies. So had Cassandra.

So had Robert. And, knowing my role, I gallantly stepped between them. "CASSIE! ROBERT! CASSIE!"

I caught a couple blows myself, but nothing on the face (after all, we had a scene to film that evening). Finally, I managed to separate them. "Cassie!" I shouted. "Listen to me! Listen!"

Another blow or two.

"Listen to me!"

She slowed to a stop, gasping, shuddering with every breath.

"I'm sure Robert doesn't know about the gaffers."

"The what?" he asked.

"The fact that the gaffers are wearing leather gloves."

"What?"

"That they are wearing *leather* gloves ... as in *cow* skin ... as in the skin of *dead animals*."

Suddenly the lights came on, and just as suddenly his incredulity. "Nuts!" he repeated. "Certifiably nuts!"

Cassandra lunged for him again, but this time I managed to catch her. I appreciated that I could hold her back, an obvious consideration on her part.

"And,"—I continued—"if you *had* known that, you would *never* have allowed them on the set."

"Michael, what are you—"

"Given your contractual obligation to ensure that no animals would be hurt in connection with the making of this film ... your *signed* obligation."

"They're leather gloves, for crying out—"

"Which can easily be replaced by heavy-duty *cloth* gloves"—I gave an exaggerated nod—"which you can pick up at any hardware store or Home Depot in less than twenty minutes so we can get back to work and not have any more *downtime*, which means not losing any more *money*."

The last phrase did it. Suddenly we were on the same page. Robert coughed, clearing his voice, "Yes, of course, certainly ... we could pick up a couple cases of *cloth* gloves and get rolling"—he glanced at his watch—"in no time."

"After you dispose of the leather ones," I said.

"Yes . . . right, after we dispose of the leather ones."

I felt the tension drain from Cassandra's body. Come to think of it, I felt it drain from my own as well. A solution had been found. Peace had been made. Sanity restored.

Well, two out of three wasn't bad.

CHAPTER 3

I stepped out of Cassandra's trailer feeling pretty good about myself for a change—at least when it came to the Sermon and its second set of "Blessed are yous." It wasn't easy, but somehow I'd pulled it off. Of course, I still wasn't buying what Annie had said about the first set—that I was *poor in spirit,* and *meek,* and *hungry.* But I hadn't done too bad a job with this second group.

The best I could tell, I really had been:

—*Merciful,* at least when it came to helping out Cassandra (who'd been high maintenance throughout the shoot) and Robert (who wasn't much better).

—*Pure in heart.* Like I said, it would have been to my advantage to walk from the problem, watch the production close down, and quietly collect my salary.

—*Peacemaker.* It looked like things were patched up and we'd be back on schedule in no time.

Of course I knew this was a bit self-congratulatory, and I didn't expect heaven to break into a standing ovation. But, who knows—if you sucked it up and really bore down, maybe the Sermon on the Mount was actually possible to live.

Unfortunately, I'd barely stepped outside when I realized we weren't quite finished. The air was filled with tension. Crew members I usually joked with averted their gaze as I approached. Conversations suddenly grew hushed or stopped altogether. I was no fool. I'd been around enough to know something was up.

"What's going on?" I asked Robert. "What's happening?"

"Happening?" he repeated.

I threw a look over at the producer and director's chairs behind the playback monitors. Everything was deserted. No surprise; after all, everyone had broken for dinner. Still, things were just a little too quiet. I took the plunge and asked, "You said Buchanan didn't like the rewrites?"

"I didn't say that."

I gave him a look.

He tried to avoid it, but couldn't. "I don't want to get in the middle of this thing, okay? This is between you and Buchanan. Whatever you two decide is fine with me."

Robert's bravery was unparalleled. I'd just saved his rear in Cassandra's trailer and thirty seconds later he was only too happy to avoid returning the favor. Corporate courage at its finest. Whether it's making movies or sweeping streets, I suppose you can always rely on somebody in midmanagement to duck and cover.

Robert cleared his throat. "Look, it's just better if your agent explains it, that's all." He cranked up his producer's grin. "Trust me on this, Michael."

Now I knew I was in trouble. Before I could respond, he invented something to shout at a production assistant about, "Hey, moron! Yes, I'm talking to *you!*" and veered away, continuing his diversionary browbeating.

It was then that I realized what everyone already knew—a battle between the superpowers was about to take place. And Robert, like everybody else, wanted to avoid contamination by being as far from the blast site as possible.

Feeling the dread of a "shoot-out" tightening my gut, I turned toward my dressing room. Wardrobe was already outside waiting. I greeted them and we entered. Swiftly and somewhat silently, they fitted me with a different swimming suit for the upcoming love scene. When they'd finished I couldn't tell any difference, but they seemed pleased, so I pretended to be. I had to. I figured I'd need all the allies I could get.

The love scene had been a bone of contention from the beginning. A deal breaker. We didn't sign on until the producers had agreed to change it from an "R" *panting-grunting-and-groping-in-the-wild-surf* scene to a more tender, *I-respect-you-too-much-to-take-advantage-of-you-in-your-moment-of-vulnerability* "PG" kiss.

In pre-production, everybody had agreed it would be "magic," "beautiful," "cinema history"—but nobody seemed to be getting around to the rewrites. Despite my repeated requests, they just didn't come in ... until last night. That's when the temperamental Buchanan exploded on the set, saying he'd never agreed to such pabulum and sent the writers back for another rewrite ... the one I had approved this morning, and the one his assistants were scurrying up and down the beach to retrieve. And now the showdown was about to begin.

The dietician brought in my dinner. I knew Charlie would be anything but thrilled with my 550-calorie (not 510, not 590, but 550) low-carb, low-fat, low-taste feast, so I sent him out with Jimmy, my personal assistant, to grab something with the rest of the crew in the buffet line. After that, they were to talk to the assistant director and get him in as background talent. Although he still didn't speak, Charlie was practically dancing in delight as they left my trailer.

After they were gone, I took a few minutes to relax and prepare myself for whatever was coming. I crossed over to the bookcase and pulled down the Bible. I found a seat, flipped to the next portion of the Sermon and read:

> *"Blessed are those who are persecuted because of righteousness, for theirs is the kingdom of heaven. Blessed are you when people insult you, persecute you and falsely say all kinds of evil against you because of me. Rejoice and be glad, because great is your reward in heaven, for in the same way they persecuted the prophets who were before you."*

For me, the concern in this section had always been the word *"falsely"* as in *"falsely"* persecuted. Whenever I take heat for my faith, I ask myself, am I really taking it *"falsely"*? Am I really standing up for something because it's right, or am I simply parading my piety, looking for opportunities to flaunt my faith?

There was a knock at the door. "Michael, it's me, can I come in?"

Me, of course, was Kenneth Halvstein, my agent. Ten years my junior—blonde, tan, almost as handsome as he was ambitious. In the seven years we'd worked together, he'd always shown tremendous business savvy and was currently considered one of the town's "young lions."

"Where are we at with Buchanan?" I asked.

"You know?"

"Meisner gave me the heads up."

"It's going to get bloody. He's digging in. He may even force you to play your religion card."

"My 'religion card'? How?"

Kenneth shrugged.

"Come on, Kenny. It's not like I'm demanding we turn the scene into a sermon. I'm not preaching Jesus or anything."

"Actually, we insisted they take out the 'J' word." (In town, no one refers to Jesus by name. He's always "the J word.")

"As cussing, sure. Tell me, why is it we only hear His name when it's used in swearing?"

"Please," Kenny raised a hand. "Let's not get into that again."

"But—"

He sighed in frustration, "For the same reason we only show evangelicals as backwoods bigots or hypocrites. It sells tickets. Now can we stay on topic?"

I ran a hand over my face. "Look, this isn't new. The script changes have been in the contract since the beginning."

Kenny nodded and moved toward the window. "It doesn't matter," he said, pulling back the curtains.

"What are you talking about? Of course it matters."

"Not tonight."

"What?"

"You might want to take a look at this."

I rose and crossed to the window to join him.

"See the photographers out there?" he asked.

I saw two or three persons with still cameras waiting at the end of the buffet line. "Aren't they with us?"

"Not those fellows."

"Buchanan let the media on the set? Why?"

"You're a bright boy, Michael. You tell me."

I frowned. Colin Buchanan was always secretive about his productions, even keeping the studio reps off-set when possible. In fact, just last week he had ferreted and threw out a "suit" who was trying to go incognito with an unshaven face and baseball cap. Why would he be inviting outsiders tonight? Unless . . . I began to see the light. "You think he's setting me up?"

"We are talking Colin Buchanan, aren't we?"

"But . . . ," I stuttered, "that's insane."

"Or genius," Kenny said, letting the curtains fall back into place.

I looked at him, waiting for more.

"Run the scene to the end, Michael. That's why they're out there, now. He's hoping you'll see the endgame before it's too late."

"Are you telling me this is a bluff?"

"No, it's a threat."

I looked at him, not understanding.

He continued. "You tell me—who has the most to lose if the two of you have a shoot-out in front of the media? A respected director, who simply wants his actor to play a scene every American hunk plays in every American film . . . or some preachy, fundamentalist actor who is afraid to show a little skin?"

I could only stare at him. I closed my eyes, then shifted them to the Bible on the table . . . recalling the words I'd read not three minutes earlier.

"Michael?"

I looked back at him.

"Michael, I've always said we're walking a tightrope with this religious thing. They've been building you up as Mr. Morality, the squeaky-clean good guy, for years. That's old news. Now they want something new, a different angle. They want dirt."

"But—"

"Imagine, Michael T. Steel, getting into a hissy fit with his director over a simple, run-of-the-mill romance scene." He reached for a grape from the table's fruit bowl. "It would definitely smack of self-righteousness; maybe even an out-of-control ego."

"*Out-of-control ego?*"

"Front page headline for the rags." He popped the grape into his mouth. "And with the Academy votes coming in . . . well, you tell me which of the two of you this is going to hurt."

I saw it now and slowly began to nod. "He's good. Very good."

"The best." Kenny reached for another grape as his cell phone chirped. He whipped it out and demanded. "Yeah?" Then, "You sure?"

The base of my skull began to ache. Confusion, anger, betrayal— you name it, I was feeling it.

"And this just in."

I looked at Kenny as he closed the phone.

"*Entertainment Tonight* is on its way."

"TV too?"

"Yup."

I took a deep breath and let it out.

Grabbing another grape, he tossed it into his mouth and headed for the door. "I'll see what I can do to head them off." He pushed it open, then turned back to me. "It's your call, Michael. I'll back you, whatever you decide. Just remember, we've worked long and hard to get where we're at. The finish line is just ten days away. With the Oscar in your pocket, you can call any shot you want."

I nodded.

"But we're not there yet, my friend." With that, he stepped out and shut the door.

I stood in the trailer, closing my eyes and rubbing my neck. I moved across the room to the table where my uneaten dinner lay. My uneaten dinner and my open Bible. What was going on? What was I doing? Was I really holding to my convictions . . . or was I shoving them down people's throats? Was I doing this because it was the right thing, or because, as the press occasionally hinted, I thought I was somehow superior? I almost smiled at that last thought—the irony of being accused of feeling superior, when I was the one who thought I needed a Savior.

I pressed my eyes. The situation was no different from what any other businessperson faces. Or homemaker. Or student. If I compromised and did the original scene, what would happen? Not much. No one would get hurt. I'd simply be doing the type of scene all my peers did. So what was the big deal?

Again, I thought of the Bible. And, almost dreading to look, I dropped my eyes to the page in front of me and continued to read:

> *"You are the salt of the earth. But if the salt loses its saltiness, how can it be made salty again? It is no longer good for anything, except to be thrown out and trampled by men."*

The phrase cut deep. I remembered a sermon from long ago, saying how salt has two properties. The first is to bring out the hidden flavors of surrounding ingredients. The second is to preserve and stop whatever is around it from decaying. I understood the part of bringing out the best in others. In my personal life and at work that part was fun, even rewarding.

But this business of stopping decay . . .

What did Annie say? *"Millions watch you and want to be like you—don't you think that's an influence?"*

She was right, of course. There were hundreds of studies proving the effect we media folk have upon others. Some even claim we have more power than the church, synagogue, school, and parents *combined.* If that's true and if, because of my compromise, even one person was influenced to have premarital sex, well then, maybe . . . I took another breath and let it out.

There was more to read, and I continued.

> *"You are the light of the world. A city on a hill cannot be hidden. Neither do people light a lamp and put it under a bowl. Instead they put it on its stand, and it gives light to everyone in the house. In the same way, let your light shine before men, that they may see your good deeds and praise your Father in heaven."*

Once again I closed my eyes. I had my answer, though I didn't like it. Not one bit. For better or worse, I was on a hilltop. And, for better or worse, I had to shine . . . hoping my "good deeds" would not be interpreted as pious self-righteousness.

There was a tap on my door.

My chest tightened.

"Mr. Steel?"

I swallowed. "Yes?"

"You're wanted on the set."

— — —

"Cut, cut, cut!"

Cassandra released a shiver she'd been holding back during the take. As best we figured, the water temperature hovered in the mid-sixties and standing there in waist-deep surf for take after take after take was anything but pleasant. "What is it this time?" she whispered to me between chattering teeth.

"I'm sure we'll find out," I said, seeing no need to whisper. The mic boom was just feet above us, picking up everything we said and feeding it directly into Colin Buchanan's headphones—Colin Buchanan, who sat warmly bundled in a padded seat at the end of the Chapman Crane sticking out over the water. Colin Buchanan, who hovered over us like God (whom more than one cast and crew member mistook him for).

"You're right, Michael," he called, "you certainly will find out what's wrong."

Cassandra let go another burst of shivers. I wrapped my arm around her shoulders. I was sad to smell the booze on her breath, no doubt from the vodka-injected orange slices her assistant kept passing to her between takes. Rumor was that Cassandra had been in and out of rehab for years. To her credit, she had managed to stay clean during the shoot ... until now. Now, her frayed nerves, her overwhelming insecurities, and the numbing cold had taken their toll.

We'd been in the water most of the evening, first shooting the scene where I rescued her. That had been easy. Four takes with two cameras and we nailed it. But it was this last setup, the very end of the sequence, that was taking so long. It was this last shot that we had been doing take after take of for the last several hours. Eventually I understood. It was an old trick, one frequently used to break younger, egocentric actors. It's amazing how forty, fifty, sixty takes can not-so-subtly remind an actor who the real boss is. The fact that Buchanan was using the trick on me made the insult greater. The fact that Cassie was an innocent pawn made it outrageous.

"I don't know ..." He spoke through the megaphone now, so everyone could hear. "It still has a certain, how should I put it ... amateurishness."

Cassandra stiffened as if she'd been slapped. I felt it too, but I wouldn't show it. I would not let him push me into a shoot-out. Not now. Not here. Not when, behind us on the beach, fifty to sixty crew, extras, and media reps stood watching ... and waiting.

Fighting to keep my voice even amidst the cold and the anger, I called, "What exactly would you like different, Colin?"

Again the bullhorn clicked. "I don't know, Michael. I just need something that's the slightest bit believable." I felt my ears growing hot and my face redden as his rebuke echoed back and forth against the beach and pier. "Perhaps, more along the lines of what we had originally scripted—something with a shred of realism, instead of this, I don't know, this drivel that you've insisted we film."

The surf splashed around our waists as Cassandra's assistant (wearing a wet suit) sloshed over and slipped her another orange slice.

"What do you think, Michael?" Buchanan continued. "You're the expert!"

What I thought was that maybe Kenny was right. Maybe I was making a mountain out of a molehill. I glanced at Cassandra, sucking away on her orange. Poor thing. How long could I make her suffer for what may be nothing more than an exercise of self-righteousness? And what about the crew? I turned to look at them on the beach. They certainly had friends and family they'd prefer to be spending a Saturday evening with. How long would I force them to stand and wait? It was one, small scene; thirty seconds, max. Maybe I *was* being overbearing with my beliefs. Maybe I *should* stop being so concerned with my precious reputation. After all, it really wasn't me, it was just a character. Just make-believe. Surely, people could tell the difference between reality and make-be—

That's when I spotted Charlie. He'd been playing a son, walking on the beach between two other extras who played his parents. I continued to stare. How many Charlies were out there? Children, teens, even adults, who built their morals, made their life choices, on what they saw in the movies? How many, for better or worse, looked up to, or even wanted to imitate, Chad Slayter, NSA? According to box office revenue and daily fan mail, thousands.

I took a deep breath, partially for warmth, partially for resolve. Then I turned to Buchanan and answered, "No, Colin, you're the boss. We'll keep doing the scene for you, just as you approved it, until you're happy."

He gave no expression, but I could tell he realized we were going to play this to the end. "As you wish, Michael," he replied. "As you wish." He nodded to the first assistant who stood in the water just below him.

"All right, people," the assistant shouted through another megaphone, "first positions, please! First positions!"

There was a noticeable sigh as cast and crew headed for their starting places at the beginning of the shot.

"Come on, folks, let's try to get out of here by morning. First positions, please. Let's move, let's move!"

I stole a glance at Buchanan, who had momentarily ordered the crane to drop to the assistant's level. He pointed toward Charlie and his "parents," asking the assistant a question. The assistant answered, motioning in my direction. Buchanan seemed to understand and nodded, not taking his eyes from them as the crane rose back into the air. I felt uneasy, but I wasn't sure why.

"Okay, everybody," the assistant shouted, "settle in, please! Settle in!"

I turned to face Cassandra. Makeup was adjusting her strands of wet hair as wardrobe repositioned her body into the skimpy bikini top. I could see her eyes were getting blurry from the booze, but she had no dialogue to deliver so it was unlikely she'd have a problem. "You okay?" I asked.

"Couldn't be better," she grinned.

"Stand by!" The assistant called.

I obediently placed my hands around her waist. She looked up, giving me a sloppy, somewhat seductive smile. Well, at least she wasn't suffering from the cold.

"Roll camera!"

"Rolling!" a voice shouted from atop the crane.

"Sound?"

"Speed," a faint voice cried from shore.

"Marker!"

A kid with the slate appeared at our side, "Devil's Breath, 115 B, take 38!" He disappeared as quickly as he had appeared.

"And . . ." It was Buchanan's voice now. "Action!"

Cassandra took a beat, then as she had so many times before, threw her arms around me, pulling my mouth to hers and kissing me passionately—until, on cue, I gently pulled away.

She looked up at me, confused, longingly, just as she had the last thirty-seven times.

And I answered, just as I had the last thirty-seven times. "Not now, Jamie. Not like this." Bending down, I gently and tenderly kissed her on the forehead. "Not like this."

I held her a moment, waiting, until we heard:

"And cut! Print that one!" Buchanan yelled. "We've got it!"

The cast and crew cheered as I felt relief wash through me.

"Okay, kids," Buchanan called, "go in and warm up while I check it on video."

With a squeal of delight, Cassandra gave me another hug and kiss, perhaps a bit too intimately, before she spun around to her assistant who caught her from falling. Together they headed back to shore. I followed. Although I was grateful to be through the ordeal, I was still suspicious. Buchanan was more cunning than this. Surely he had something else up his sleeve.

Unfortunately, I couldn't have been more right.

– – –

"WHERE IS HE?!"

I looked up from toweling off. Buchanan had been standing at the video assist monitors surveying the playback of the last take. Everyone had been moving about, preparing to call it a night. Until now . . .

"WHERE IS THE KID WHO RUINED MY SHOT?!"

Cast, crew, extras, everyone froze. They may have glanced at one another but no one was foolish enough to let their eyes meet Buchanan's, lest he needed a suitable proxy.

I glanced about and noticed that Robert Meisner had disappeared, once again performing his infamous duck and cover trick. Unfortunately, I was next up in the food chain and it was my job to respond. "Something wrong, Colin?"

"SOMETHING WRONG!?" he roared. "TAKE A LOOK AT THIS!"

I moved toward him, the crowd parting like the Red Sea.

"Play it back!" he shouted to the video operator. "Play it back!"

As the videotape rewound, Buchanan screamed at his nearest assistant. "Bring me the extras! I want all the extras here, and I want them here now!"

I arrived just as the slate appeared on the screen for take 38 and the action began. It was beautifully lit . . . the fake moonlight sparkling off the water, Cassandra and me kissing, the beach and city in the background.

"There!" he pointed to the faint forms walking along the beach—Charlie and his two parents. "He's looking at the camera! The brat is looking straight at my camera!"

I leaned toward the monitor, staring at the image. The three dots were barely visible.

"Where are they!?" he demanded of no one in particular. "Bring them to me!"

"They're on their way, Mr. Buchanan," someone called.

I squinted at the screen. "Colin, they're fifty yards away. You can barely see them. How can you—"

"Are you telling me how to direct my picture!?"

"Of course not, but—"

"If I say he's looking at my camera, he's looking at my camera!"

"Here they are, Mr. Buchanan."

He spun around, pointing and glaring—not at the parents, but directly at Charlie. "YOU!" With a series of oaths, he continued. "YOU HAVE DESTROYED MY SHOT!!"

The parents instinctively shrank back, leaving Charlie exposed and on his own.

"WE HAVE BEEN HERE ALL NIGHT! AND NOW WE MUST GO OUT AND DO IT ALL OVER AGAIN!"

Charlie wilted under the rage, confused, terrified.

"AND IT IS ALL YOUR FAULT!"

I quickly stepped to the boy's side. "Come on, Colin." Charlie threw his arms around me, clinging in fear. "He's just a kid."

"HE'S AN IDIOT! AN IGNORANT IDIOT WHO HAS RUINED AN ENTIRE EVENING'S WORK!"

Somewhere in the back of my mind, I knew what was coming down, but there was nothing I could do to stop it—not and defend Charlie. I motioned to the monitor. "You can't even see their faces. How can you—"

"Who are you to tell me what I can or can't—"

"Look at the screen, Colin!" I was getting hot.

"You want to direct this picture, Mr. Steel!?"

"I want you to be a human being and look at the—"

"Throwing your weight around may intimidate others, but it doesn't impress me."

"Nobody's throwing their weight around!" A TV light glared on. The whir-click of an autowind camera began. Charlie clung tighter, burying his face into my side. I fought to bring it down a notch. "Listen, Colin . . . I'm just trying to put this thing in perspective."

"Perspective!?"

"Yes. The bottom line here, the reality of the situation is—"

"*Reality!?* Who are you to talk to me about reality!?"

"I'm just—"

"You, who insists, who *demands*, that a healthy man and a beautiful woman in love will not make love. You call that *reality?*"

"They're not married," I exclaimed.

Another TV light flared on.

"*Not married?!*" Buchanan shouted. "*Not married?!* The reality, Mr. Steel, in case you haven't noticed, is that this is the twenty-first century! People have sex *before* they're married. That's reality! A reality that you in your little Pollyanna make-believe world are afraid to show!"

That was it. He'd pushed the buttons. "Reality?" I jabbed my finger at him—an unfortunate pose that sent any remaining cameras whirring and clicking. "You want reality? Good, then let's do your sex scene. But let's really show reality!"

The crowd shifted, stunned.

Buchanan played them, "That is all I ask."

"I mean let's *really* show what happens!" I shouted. "Let's really show the reality of the morning after, when hearts are spent and broken and empty."

"Oh, please—"

"No, I'm serious! Let's really show the reality of getting a sexually transmitted disease, or dying of AIDS. You want reality, then let's show it. But let's show all of it!"

Buchanan made a face, mocking me. My vision narrowed, my heart pounded. TV lights and cameras were everywhere, but it no longer mattered.

"Or let's have her get pregnant and raise the child on her own! Let's make the father a deadbeat dad so she has to hold down two jobs. Or maybe take her through the trauma of an abortion—yeah, that would be good, wouldn't it? Show the whole thing, and make sure you capture the emotional scars she may never recover from." I moved in so close we were practically face to face—a photographer's dream. "You want reality, Buchanan, then let's show reality. But let's show *all* of it!"

He stared at me, giving his jaw muscles a workout. For the briefest moment he faltered, unsure how to respond. I'd taken the wind from his sails, left him defenseless, given him only one recourse. And he took it. "GET OFF MY SET!" he yelled.

"With pleasure!" I spun around, placing my hand on Charlie's shoulder and guiding him through the crowd. TV cameras jostled, lights glared, cameras whirred.

"This is *my* set!" Buchanan shouted. "MY set!! And I won't have you cram your narrow-minded, religious dogma down any of our throats. Do you hear me? DO YOU HEAR ME?!"

Charlie and I made our way across the sand toward the parking lot. Off to the left I saw Brad, my driver, scrambling, trying to reach the limo before me. He didn't have to worry. I had a slight delay.

"Mr. Steel?" A young man in Dockers, tie, and backpack approached.

I was in no mood to talk, especially to a fan. But he was no fan.

"Mr. Steel, please?" He held out an envelope.

Trying to maintain some civility, I obliged and took it. "What is this?" I asked.

"You've just been served divorce papers."

CHAPTER 4

CHAPTER 4
CHAPTER 4
CHAPTER 4
CHAPTER 4

What was it Annie had said? *"We all have our battlefronts."* I knew the situation between Buchanan and myself was no different than that of any other employee asked to compromise their beliefs by their boss. And the situation with my wife? What are the statistics now, one out of two marriages end up in the dumpster? I looked out the window at the passing ocean as the moon highlighted its breaking surf. I swallowed back the tightness in my throat. The situations may be no different, but the pain was no less.

Tanya and I had been college sweethearts, married right out of UCLA. Together we endured those early, macaroni-and-cheese days, the poverty actually drawing us closer. We were inseparable, the model couple, the envy of all our friends.

The first bumps came with the miscarriages. After the tests we learned that we'd never be able to go full term with a baby. Of course there were other options, but not then, not with our income. I'll never forget the afternoon we learned. We held each other on into the night, crying, wiping each other's tears, vowing that our love for one another was enough, that all we needed was to grow old together in each other's arms. And it was true. For a while. Until success started.

I'll be the first to take blame, at least in the beginning. When you're at work with people who start catering to your every whim, who begin treating you like the fourth part of the Trinity, then come home to be yelled at for not cleaning the cat box—well, it takes a bit of practice to go through that kind of decompression on a daily basis.

But we adjusted. There were more potholes along the way, but we adjusted. Things only got ugly when Chad Slayter came onto the scene as some sort of sex symbol, a devoted-to-God-and-country hunk (it's amazing what they can do with lighting and camera angles). As you can imagine, it was hard for Tanya seeing bimbos stuff underwear into my coat pocket, or catching them sifting through our garbage, or her reading about my supposed love affairs in the tabloids . . . complete with digitally doctored photos. For the record, though I was tempted more times than I care to remember, I remained faithful.

Still, I suppose there are other types of unfaithfulness. In my case it was trying to stay on board a skyrocketing career with its relentless demands, its filming around the world, its continual scrutiny under the public spotlight. For Tanya, it was her seduction into high society, socializing with influential people we didn't like, impressing them with purchases we didn't need. Days and then weeks went by when our schedules didn't even permit us to see one another. Gradually, our lives grew more separate. That's when the fights began, the frustrations, the miscommunication. Eventually we found ourselves sleeping in separate bedrooms. And, for the past nine weeks, she had been staying at a rented condo in Brentwood. She said it was to be closer to her work (she was a volunteer at the Getty), that the commute on Pacific Coast Highway was just too brutal. A surprise visit by me, complete with flowers, indicated it might have more to do with the interior designer she was dining with than with rush-hour traffic. We tried counseling with our pastor, but there were just too many forces driving and pulling us apart. We had finally achieved the American dream—which in reality had become an American nightmare.

I glanced at the divorce papers in my hand, then leaned back and closed my eyes. I could hear Charlie playing with the switches and controls beside me. If he was enamored by Robert's Lexus, he was enthralled with the limo. Refrigerator, entertainment center, you name it, he was exploring it. I'd already called Annie. She said it was cool to bring him home, just as long as I stayed in touch.

I opened my eyes. Now he was investigating the TV. "The remote's over there," I said, pointing to the console.

He scooped it up and snapped it on. Instantly, an all-too-familiar voice came over the speakers:

"Do not think that I have come to abolish the La-aw or the Prophets."

"Oh no . . . ," I groaned.

I stared in unbelief at the picture. The preacher was a sweating, overfed gentleman, stuffed into a cheap suit with a shirt collar two sizes too small.

"I have not come to abolish them but to fulfill them."

"Turn it off!" I pleaded. "Turn it off!"

Charlie fumbled with the remote and changed channels. But all he got was static. He tried the next channel. More static. And the next, and the next, and the next, until we were back to the preacher.

"I tell you the truth, until heaven and earth disappear, not the small-est letter, not the least stroke of a pen, will by any means disappear from the La-aw until everything is accomplished."

I pressed the intercom for the driver. "Brad?"

"Sir?" came the voice.

"What's wrong with the TV? We're only getting one channel."

"I just had it serviced. Are you sure?"

"Of course I'm sure. All we're getting is some late-night religious thing."

"I'll look into it, Mr. Steel. Just as soon as I get back."

"Please?" I begged.

"Yes, sir."

I released the button and continued staring at the screen in disbelief. Does this guy ever give it a rest? I thought of ordering Charlie to turn it off, but we had a twenty-five minute ride up the coast before we got home and he was enjoying the novelty of it, so . . .

"Anyone who breaks one of the least of these commandments and teaches others to do the same will be called least in the kingdom of

heaven, but whoever practices and teaches these commands will be called great in the kingdom of heaven. For I tell you that unless your righteousness surpasses that of the Pharisees and the teachers of the la-aw, you will certainly not enter the kingdom of heaven."

I shook my head—not only at the coincidence, but the content. All of my life I had been taught that Christ came to give us freedom and peace. What's the verse about His yoke being "easy" and His burden "light"? But then He turns around with something like this. How could trying to follow all of these commands be interpreted as *easy*? How could sinking under their impossible weight be *light*?

It certainly wasn't for me.

Aren't we told that Christ came to *free* us from the Law? Well, this sure didn't sound like freedom. In truth, it sounded like He was piling on even more rules.

"You have heard that it was said to the people long ago, 'Do not murder, and anyone who murders will be subject to judgment.' But I tell you that anyone who is angry with his brother will be subject to judgment. Again, anyone who says to his brother, 'Raca,' is answerable to the Sanhedrin. But anyone who says, 'You fool!' will be in danger of the fire of hell."

I thought of my anger toward Buchanan. How was it possible *not* to be angry? *Not* to hate? With all of the world's meanness, cruelty, and injustice, how was it possible for anyone? And to insist that anger was akin to murder? That by calling your enemy a fool, you put yourself in danger of hell? Who could follow such rules!? I glanced back down at the papers in my hand. I wasn't supposed to resent these?

Once again I felt the guilt piling up—the helplessness of not being able to obey, of not pleasing God. I stared at the screen as the back of my throat ached.

"Therefore, if you are offering your gift at the altar and there remember that your brother has something against you, leave your gift there in front of the altar. First go and be reconciled to your brother; then come and offer your gift."

He expects us to make things right with others before we even go to Him? How was that possible? How could it be done?!

"Settle matters quickly with your adversary who is taking you to court. Do it while you are still with him on the wa-ay, or he may hand you over to the judge, and the judge may hand you over to the officer, and you may be thrown into prison. I tell you the truth, you will not get out until you have paid the last penny."

Of course Buchanan and I would make up. With a 90-million-dollar picture at stake, we had to. Like any office blow out, we'd patch up things. I looked back at the papers. The same was true with Tanya. We would be civil. Respectful. We had no choice.

But not to be angry? Not to be resentful? To be more righteous than the scribes and Pharisees? How was that possible? Unless there was something I was missing, something deeper . . .

But what?

I glanced over at Charlie. He had already lost interest and was looking out the window. Good. I reached for the TV remote and shut it off.

Ah, silence. Blessed, peaceful silence.

At least on the outside. But inside I was staggering under Christ's impossible demands. And, when I wasn't staggering, I was feeling very helpless, very angry . . . and very abandoned.

– – –

I'd just gotten Charlie to bed in the guest room, the one with the glass wall overlooking the pool and beach. Tomorrow was Sunday and, if he was interested, I'd promised him a swim, church, and a walk up the beach before taking him back to the city. He *was* interested. Very interested. Especially about the beach. He seemed to have bounced back pretty well from Buchanan's assault. For that I was grateful. He still hadn't talked, but I figured tomorrow was another day. Besides, it was late and he was exhausted. In fact, his head had barely hit the pillow before he was out.

Wish I could say the same for me. After showering, I slipped on a robe and tried to find something to read. With a half-dozen screenplays to consider, I had more than enough. But nothing held my interest. Nothing except . . . listen, I'm not superstitious or anything, but something was definitely going on with this Sermon. I mean the dreams, the televangelist picking up exactly where he'd left off, the way each section seemed to unfold right when I was living it. I don't care how it sounds, but everything was feeling just a bit too coincidental. So, like a moth drawn to the flame, I crossed to the bed and found myself reaching for the Bible on the nightstand. And why not? If something else was coming down, it wouldn't hurt to have a little heads up beforehand.

I flipped the pages, found my place, and continued:

"You have heard that it was said, 'Do not commit adultery.' But I tell you that anyone who looks at a woman lustfully has already committed adultery with her in his heart."

I'd known this concept since puberty. I mused how later, at men's retreats, we proved our piety by looking the other way when beautiful women floated past. There was nothing wrong with our attempts, but even then I knew there was a world of difference between appreciating beauty and "looking lustfully." What was it Martin Luther had said about sin being like birds? It's not a problem if they land in our branches; that's only normal. Even Jesus was faced with temptation. The problem comes when we don't shake them away, when we let the thoughts linger and start building nests.

"If your right eye causes you to sin, gouge it out and throw it away. It is better for you to lose one part of your body than for your whole body to be thrown into hell. And if your right hand causes you to sin, cut it off and throw it away. It is better for you to lose one part of your body than for your whole body to go into hell."

Harsh words. But, to be honest, I've seen the agony of other Christian men who have been trapped by the drug of pornography. Many have never been able to get free of it. I imagine in some ways the hell of their addiction is no worse than this eternal hell Christ spoke of.

I hesitated to read on. I knew what was coming next and had no desire to continue. But, if I was serious about the Sermon and trying to live it, I knew it was a package deal. All or nothing. I couldn't pick and choose. So I kept reading . . .

"It has been said, 'Anyone who divorces his wife must give her a certificate of divorce.' But I tell you that anyone who divorces his wife, except for marital unfaithfulness, causes her to become an adulteress, and anyone who marries the divorced woman commits adultery."

I closed my eyes. This was a tough one, especially today. And, of course, with women now viewed as equal to men in our justice system, it cut both ways. So what was I to do? Play the legalistic waiting game? Hope Tanya hurried up and had sex with her designer friend, thereby making her unfaithful, thereby freeing me to run off and remarry? It seemed like a bit of a legal loophole.

Or was Jesus once again saying something deeper? Was He referring to a greater problem, one to which the loophole was only a Band-Aid?

I gave a start at the security gate buzzer. This time of night, it was probably kids playing pranks. Still, just in case, I reached for the TV remote and clicked on the security channel. A silver Jaguar appeared on the screen.

"Michael . . ."

I switched to the closer camera and saw Cassandra shouting at the speaker. She looked no more sober than she had earlier. "Michael . . . Michael?"

I pressed the *Enter* button on the remote. The driveway lights glared on and the black, iron gate silently opened. As she drove in, I noticed a car parked across the road but I paid little attention. It could have been part of her entourage, perhaps a bodyguard or, just as likely, some couple with no other place to make out.

I adjusted my robe and, still in bare feet, padded along the hallway. I arrived at the sweeping staircase and headed downstairs. Her car door slammed as I entered the marble entry hall. I flipped on the chandelier, unlatched the locks and swung open the door just as she arrived. She wore one of those expensive grey Burberry London overcoats. "Cassie," I asked, "are you okay?"

She slowed to a stop, smiling a sloppy grin.

I opened the door wider, "Please, come in. Is everything all right? Are you okay? Did something—"

That's when she threw her arms around my neck and kissed me. For a moment I was stunned. Then, for another moment I felt myself enjoying it; the warmth and touch of another person. The evening had been very difficult and I was feeling very alone. Alone and betrayed by everyone, including God.

We separated and I caught my breath, recovering. Well, sort of.

"Wow," I said, trying to make light as I shut the door behind her, "what was that about?"

"Just look upon it as a thank you." Her speech wasn't slurred, but close.

"You drove all the way out here to say thanks?"

"You came to my defense, Michael, against Robert." She looked up, her green eyes locking onto mine. "I don't take that lightly."

"Yes, well, I—"

"I saw what Buchanan did to you. And I heard about your wife."

"Good news travels fast."

Taking a step closer, she lowered her voice, "She's a fool."

I knew what I should do, but I was paralyzed. Still holding my eyes, she raised onto her toes and again kissed me—tenderly at first, but it soon grew in intensity. And, as ashamed as I am to admit it, I returned the kiss, matching her passion with my own, letting go my defenses, giving in. I was so alone and she was so . . . present.

To Cassie's defense, she took my response as permission to continue. Silently, she reached down and unbuckled her coat, so stealthily that I barely knew it until I heard the material crumple to the floor. Then I opened my eyes and saw her, nearly naked, save for the skimpiest Frederick's of Hollywood undergarments.

And still the kiss continued. Yes, alarms were going off. Yes, warning lights flashed. But it felt so good to be with someone, anyone, especially with so much affection . . . and hunger. Desire continued welling up inside of me, drowning the guilt. After all, people did this all the time, didn't they? What would it matter? Hadn't I been the good boy? All of my life, hadn't I played by the rules? And look where it got me.

I felt her hands reach up and untie my robe.

So alone. So cut off. And now here was someone to be with, someone to touch and hold, someone to share the evening.

She slipped her arms around my back, drawing our bodies closer, skin against skin, flesh against flesh . . . and then, and then . . . I can't explain it, really. It wasn't like I heard a voice, or even felt an impression. At that particular moment, I wasn't even feeling guilt. No, this was different. It was . . . a realization. A realization even greater than the hunger that filled me.

Suddenly I understood that I was . . . *betraying*, that was the word. I was *betraying* a friend. But not my wife. No, this friendship was deeper. As deep as who I was. I was betraying a commitment, a love. Something so rich, so important, that any desire I felt paled by comparison. And—though every cell in my body screamed *Yes!*—there was a deeper realization that quietly whispered, "No. Our love is too great for this."

And, as that gentle understanding filled me, I had the strength, the desire, to pull away.

At first Cassandra thought I was coming up for air, but when she moved in again and I shied away, she slowed to a stop and looked at me.

"Sorry," I mumbled clumsily.

Thinking I needed encouragement, she moved in again.

Again, I pulled back.

"It's okay," she whispered, "it's what we both want. What we've both wanted for so long."

I wasn't sure if she was quoting from a movie or from her life—sometimes for Cassie the boundaries blur. I reached behind me and gently removed her arms. "No," I said, as gently as possible.

She tilted her head quizzically.

I searched those deep green eyes, trying to find an explanation she would understand. "Look. You're a beautiful woman and—"

"And you're a gorgeous man—" Again her hands started around my waist and again I took them.

"No, you don't understand."

She tried one last time. "Oh, baby, I under—"

"No," I said, more firmly. Then, continuing softer, "I can't explain it."

She paused. "You think she'll come back to you," she said, endeared by what she thought was the romantic in me. "You still love her, don't you?"

I shook my head. "No, it has nothing to do with my love . . . for her." I looked away, pulling my robe together, searching the distant wall for an explanation.

"Then who?"

I continued thinking.

"Michael . . ." She was smiling, but there was an edge to her voice. "I'm not used to throwing myself at men."

I didn't know how true that was, but I nodded.

"And I'm certainly not used to being rejected."

That I did know to be accurate.

"So . . ." She started to see the picture. "There's somebody else, but it isn't your wife."

"I, uh—" I took a deep breath and blew it out. What was I to say? That I was in love with God? That by having sex with her, I was being unfaithful to Him? That I was some sort of male nun married to Christ? Somehow I doubted she'd buy it.

She threw a glance up to the bedrooms. "She'd better be incredible, Michael, because I'll tell you, I don't need this humiliation."

"I know."

"I mean if word ever got out—"

"Word will never get," I assured her.

"I have a reputation—"

"I under—"

"—an image to maintain. And if people ever knew I came all the way out here just to be—" She suddenly stopped, her eyes fixing on something up the staircase behind me.

I turned. There was little Charlie. He clung to the rail, wearing only his briefs. "Charlie, what are you doing out of bed?"

Cassandra made a little gasping sound and I turned to see her eyes darting from Charlie to me and back to Charlie again. It took a moment to realize what was going through her mind. "Cassandra," I reached for her arm, "surely you don't think—"

She yanked away, eyes still shooting back and forth, trying to find the words. Finally, she did. "You . . . *pervert*."

I tried to chuckle at the misunderstanding. "Cassie, it's not what you—"

"No wonder." She took a half step backwards toward the door, distancing herself as if I had some disease.

"Cassie—" I turned back to the boy, "Charlie, go to bed." Then back to Cassandra, who had turned and was fumbling with the door handle.

"Cass—"

"Stay away from me"—she finally got it open—"you filth!" Then, remembering her coat, she scooped it up from the floor. She didn't bother putting it on as she stepped outside. She was too shocked or disgusted or drunk, or all of the above.

"Cassandra!"

"You sick . . ." she struggled with the words. "You perverted . . . monster!"

"Cassie!"

I followed her outside. The entrance lights to the driveway still blazed as, nearly naked, she continued toward her car. "You had us all thinking you were so good, so moral!" She spun back to me, shouting, "The pious Christian who won't soil his holy hands! While all the time . . . While all the time . . ."

It was then, I spotted movement on the other side of the gate. A dark form had dashed across the road, and was pressing against the bars. There was the briefest reflection of light against glass and then a tiny pinpoint of red began to glow. A camera! Someone was videotaping!

Cassandra continued her tirade. "No man alive would turn down what I was offering you! No . . . *normal, healthy* one. But *you* . . ." Seeing I was looking at something, she spun around and spotted it as well. Quickly, she reached for her coat, struggling to find the sleeves, to slip it on.

I moved to help.

"Stay away!" she cried, still fighting the coat.

"Cassie," I kept my voice low, continuing toward her, reaching out. "It's not what it—"

She staggered back. "Keep away from me! Keep your sick, perverted hands away from me!"

Finally, getting her arms into her sleeves, she wrapped herself up and stumbled to the car.

"Cass—"

She threw open the door. Then, either getting ahold of herself, or pretending to for the camera, she cried, "If you don't want to be with a woman, that's your business, Michael. But"—she swallowed back the revulsion—"*little boys?*"

"It's not—"

"You're sick, Michael! What you're doing is sick and disgusting and illegal and . . . and sick! And you need help!" With that she slammed the door, turned on the ignition, and threw the car into reverse. Tires squealed. She barely gave the automatic gate time to open before she shot out, forcing the reporter who was still taping, to leap back.

Once outside, she slid to a stop and rolled down the window to give a parting shout—for both the camera and her reputation. "You're a sick man, Michael! You need to get help!" She shifted gears, stomped on the accelerator, and spun out, giving the photographer more dramatic footage than he ever dreamed possible.

Well, not quite.

For once she'd sped away and the gate started to close, he turned his camera back toward me standing in the driveway . . . just as little Charlie arrived and took my hand in his, wearing only his underwear.

Interlude

FADE IN:

INT. HEAVEN—DAY
The Accuser of the Brethren and the Creator are
having another debriefing.

                    GOD
          So where have you been?

                    SATAN
          Can we just cut to the chase?

                    GOD
          Talk to Me.

                    SATAN
          I like Michael. I don't want to see
          him hurt. Why not concede now before
          things get too bloody?

                    GOD
          I've never been afraid of blood. As
          you recall, it was the blood of My
          only—

                    SATAN
               [hastily interrupting]
          Listen, if You call the whole thing
          off now—

                    GOD
          "Call it off?" This is where it gets
          interesting. You saw how close he came
          to understanding it.

                    SATAN
          "It"?

                    GOD
          The key, the solution.

                    SATAN
          When?

GOD

During the kiss.

SATAN

What are You talking about? That was
my darkest moment of temptation!

GOD

Which became My brightest moment of
revelation.

SATAN

You're doing it again.

GOD

What's that?

SATAN

Defeating me with my victories.

GOD

Old habits die hard.

SATAN
[with a heavy sigh]
So You still want to continue?

GOD

Until I finish My work, yes.

SATAN

Your work? I thought it was mine.

GOD

You always do.

SATAN
[growing angry]
Listen, if we keep going, it's going
to get ugly—I promise you, it will
get very, very ugly.

GOD

Why am I not surprised? Oh, that's
right, I'm God.

```
                    SATAN
            [trying not to snarl]
        You have my word, I'm going to get
        down and dirty.

                     GOD
        So I can raise him up, whole and
        complete.

                    SATAN
        Don't blame me. I've given You fair
        warning.

                     GOD
        Yes, that's very thoughtful. Now skulk
        along, please. I've got a universe to
        run.

                                FADE OUT
```

I started awake. It was just past two in the morning. The sheets clung to my damp body as I turned and stared up at the ceiling. The dream was nearly identical to the other two, except for the change in dialogue . . . which made it all the more unnerving.

Then memories flooded in . . . the beach fight, the kiss, the scene in the driveway. And the dream again. The all too vivid dream. I groaned. There was no way I was going back to sleep. I reached for the TV remote and hit "Power." I was anxious to fill my head with something, anything, other than the dream and memories.

Well, almost anything.

Suddenly, the televangelist filled the screen:

"Again, you have heard that it was said to the people long ago, 'Do not break your oath, but keep the oaths you have made to the Lord."

I stared at the screen, my mouth sagging open. Who was this guy!?

"But I tell you, Do not swear at all: either by heaven, for it is God's throne; or by the earth, for it is his footstool; or by Jerusalem, for it is the city of the Great King. And do not swear by your head, for you cannot make even one hair white or black. Simply let your

'Yayus' be 'Yayus,' and your 'No,' 'No'; anything beyond this comes from the evil one."

I clicked it off. Enough was enough. I took a deep breath and let it out, just as the phone rang. I reached for it and fumbled with the receiver until I got it to my face. "Hello?"

"Michael?"

"Kenny, what's up?"

"You tell me. I just got a call from a friend over at Malibu P.D. They're sending a squad car to the house."

"Mine? Why?"

"Just tell me the truth; between you and me. Did you do it?"

"Do what?"

"You know, the kid ... what Cassie was ranting about?"

My mind reeled, groping to understand.

"Just tell me the truth, Mikey. You've always been a man of integrity; everyone knows that. If you say yes, we'll get you some help and we'll get through this. If you say no, I'll go to the mat with you on it. It's that simple. Yes or no, Mikey. Yes or no."

When I finally found my voice I managed to choke out, "No, of course not! Who, who would report such a thing?"

"Report?"

"Yes, who filed the report?"

"Nobody filed a report, Mikey. It's all over the news."

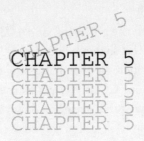

CHAPTER 5

The circus arrived at dawn. From my bedroom balcony I could see two vans parked along the road, raising their microwave towers in the early morning light. Actually, morning light seldom comes to the beach. With our fog, things just gradually grow less and less dark.

By the time I'd dressed, the number of vans had doubled with an additional half-dozen cars joining them. Celebrity perversion is big news.

In many ways the group reminded me of giant bugs—maggots swarming around the gate, sipping coffee, joking, anxious to start feeding upon the carcass. If that sounds disrespectful, it's meant to. Don't get me wrong, there are great reporters in this world and real journalism certainly has a place. But not this type of sideshow reporting. These are the folks who thrive off another's tragedy. These are the ones who shove microphones into victims' faces encouraging them to relive their nightmares for higher ratings.

I pulled away from the balcony before any telephoto lens could find me. I figured the more ambitious ones would eventually scale the fence and scamper over the lawn. Of course my security system would automatically call the police, who would eventually show up and escort them back outside with a slap on the wrist ... but not before they grabbed a few close shots. From what I'd heard with others, this was pretty much standard procedure.

I didn't have the stomach to turn on the TV. I could only imagine what scene they were playing over and over again—how it would be intercut with some reporter outside my gate, explaining that the Malibu Police had arrived earlier, interviewed me, and taken Charlie into protective custody.

That interview with the police, around 4:00 this morning, was the worst hour of my life. Not so much because of the accusation (though you can imagine how incredibly embarrassing that was), but because of the fear I saw in poor Charlie's eyes as they took him away. He never cried audibly, but tears streamed down his face as he reached for me, as they held him back, as I promised everything would be okay, as he lunged and fought, as they carried him outside and forcibly loaded him into the car.

It was an awful sight. One I'll never forget.

Of course I'd phoned Annie, and she immediately contacted Child Protective Services while preparing to head for the station to straighten things out. I'd offered to meet her there, but she didn't think much of the idea. Not that I blamed her. For now, it was important I keep a low profile.

Yeah, right.

The phone rang for the hundredth time. Though my number is unlisted, it was ringing off the hook. Thanks to Caller ID, the only ones I'd picked up were Kenny and Pastor Barbour. Oddly enough, both my agent and my pastor had reached the same conclusion: It was essential for my career (and probably my soul) that I show up for church. I understood Kenny's rationale, but was a little disappointed at my pastor's. Somehow I'd hoped he was above using God to protect and advance careers ... mine or his. That might be a bit harsh, but I've seen the most devout folks struggle with the seduction of fame. Sex, money, power—they're kid stuff. But dangle a healthy dose of fame in front of us and look out. Still, Kenny's and Pastor Barbour's counsel was solid, and I had agreed. Kenny and a bodyguard would pick me up for the early service.

I caught some movement out of the corner of my eye and turned back to the balcony. A small handful had breached the gate and were scampering across the lawn toward my bedroom. Apparently I'd been spotted.

I moved to the fireplace, out of sight, and slumped into my reading chair. The assault had begun. Actually it had never ceased, not since last night's incident on the set. No, that's not true. It had started before that—one week and one day before that—after reading and rereading the Sermon on the Mount. After vowing in this very chair that I'd try to live by its words.

I looked at the Bible on the nightstand and felt myself filling with a mixture of anger, resentment, and awe. This was far more than coincidence. It had to be. But—

I heard the faintest scrape overhead, not far from the balcony. It was followed by the sound of pottery shattering on the drive below. But it couldn't be pottery. There were no pots outside. There was nothing, but—

Another scrape. Someone was on my roof! Someone had scaled the wall of my house, climbed onto my roof, and had accidentally knocked off one of its Spanish tiles. For a moment I froze in fear, but it quickly turned to anger. How dare they! I rose, tilting my head, straining to listen. There it was again, another scrape. Directly above the balcony. The unmitigated gall!

But two could play that game. I moved across the room and quickly flattened myself against the wall.

More scraping and the mildest of gruntings. I couldn't see, but I knew he was trying to lower himself from the roof onto the landing. I waited, picturing the progress in my mind. Then, when I thought the time was just right, I leaped in front of the balcony, threw up my hands, and screamed, "BOOGA! BOOGA! BOOGA!"

All right, maybe it wasn't the cleverest of screams, but it did the trick. The reporter, a kid with a camera and a nearly terminal case of acne, let out a cry, lurched backwards and tumbled over the railing. He caught himself briefly on the wrought iron—which probably saved his life—before falling the remaining fifteen feet to the pavement below. A couple reporters moved in to make sure he was okay. Gratefully, his neck wasn't broken. Hopefully, his legs were.

Feeling the rush of victory, not to mention vindication, I glanced about my room, wondering what other foes needed vanquishing. My eyes landed on the Bible. I took a deep breath and let it out. There were still a few minutes before Kenny would arrive, so I scooped it up, headed back to my chair, and plopped down. I figured it wouldn't hurt to see what was in store for me next:

"You have heard that it was said, 'Eye for eye, and tooth for tooth.' But I tell you, Do not resist an evil person. If someone strikes you on the right cheek, turn to him the other also. And if someone wants to sue you and take your tunic, let him have your cloak as well. If someone forces you to go one mile, go with him two miles. Give to the one who asks you, and do not turn away from the one who wants to borrow from you."

I paused, closing my eyes at the frustration, the impossibility of what I read. In just the past few hours I'd acquired more than my fair share of enemies—Buchanan, Cassandra, and, of course, the scavengers below who were anxious to feed off any rumors and innuendo (or, if necessary, to create them).

I sighed wearily and looked back to the page.

"You have heard that it was said, 'Love your neighbor and hate your enemy.' But I tell you: Love your enemies and pray for those who persecute you, that you may be sons of your Father in heaven. He causes his sun to rise on the evil and the good, and sends rain on the righteous and the unrighteous. If you love those who love you, what reward will you get? Are not even the tax collectors doing that? And if you greet only your brothers, what are you doing more than others? Do not even pagans do that? Be perfect, therefore, as your heavenly Father is perfect."

I looked up, suddenly not feeling as good about the kid who fell off the balcony—even wondering if he was okay.

With a certain contempt for my softheartedness, I rose and moved to the balcony to take a peek. There they were, trampling my lawn and flowers, making idle chitchat as they littered the place with paper cups and cigarette butts. And there, off to the left, lying under the pepper tree, lay the kid. He wasn't moving much, but he had to be okay. I mean, his fellow bottom-feeders would have certainly checked him out, wouldn't they?

It was then I spotted Kenny's Mercedes turning off the highway into the drive. He stopped at the box, entered the security code, and the gate swung open—not only bringing the party on my lawn to life, but also allowing the other, less athletic members who were stranded outside to join them. Now everyone was able to participate, swarming the car, approaching my house. Everyone but the kid under the tree.

— — —

"Step back!"

"Just tell us—"

"Michael, how long have you and the boy been—"

The bodyguard growled. "I said step back!" He was a bruiser of a man covered in tattoos. He moved through the crowd like a snow-plow, allowing Kenny and me to follow in his wake.

"What's it feel like to have your dirty laundry aired before—"

"After church," Kenny shouted. "We'll have a statement for you after—"

"Surely you have some comment about—"

We arrived at the car as Bruiser opened the back door for me. I started inside but paused, half in, half out, looking over the roof, try-ing to spot the kid under the tree. I couldn't shake the feeling that something was wrong, that I had to do something. Yes, part of it was from the Scripture I'd read, but part of it was something else. Unfortunately, Bruiser didn't display the same sensitivity as he half-guided, half-threw me into the seat. He slammed the door as reporters fired off photos and videotaped me through the window. Kenny, spouting oaths of frustration, had less trouble entering the driver's seat and nobody got in Bruiser's way as he moved to the front passenger side.

Kenny motioned for the crowd to step back, revving the engine as a warning, while inching our way toward the front gate. We were about halfway there when I finally spotted him.

"Stop!" I shouted. "Stop the car!"

"What?!"

I had the same sensation as when Cassie and I were lip-locked in the entry hall—that same feeling of commitment, of loyalty. I was already opening the door. "Stop the car, stop the—"

"Michael, what are you—"

I jumped out and raced for the pepper tree.

The crowd quickly pursued, but I paid little attention as I ran across the lawn. "Are you all right?" I called to the boy.

He struggled to sit up, looking surprised and confused.

"Are you all right?" I repeated.

He nodded. Self-conscious at the sudden attention, he tried to rise. "Sure, I'm all—" until he toppled back to the grass. He grabbed his leg, embarrassed, trying not to show the pain.

I arrived and knelt down. "Here," I said, reaching for his pant leg, "let me see—"

"I'm all right," he said, pulling back. "I'm—"

"Let me see it!"

He stopped fighting and allowed me pull up his left pant leg. His ankle was nearly the size of his calf, and it was bleeding. I'm no doctor, but it looked broken. "Who's with you?" I asked.

"Huh?" Then understanding, he answered, "Nobody. I'm freelance."

"You're by yourself; there's nobody to drive you back?"

Again he tried to rise, embarrassed by the attention. "My car's just outside the—" He fell quicker this time.

I looked up at the group surrounding us and said, "His leg's broken. Can one of you drive him to the hospital?"

There was the usual clicking and whirring of autowind cameras but no volunteers.

"Can one of you drive him to Urgent Care?"

No one seemed to hear.

I shook my head in disbelief. Incredible. I turned back to the kid. "Here," I said, taking his arm, "hang on." With some effort, I finally got him to his feet. More whirring cameras. "Now, lean on me and—"

"I can do—"

"Lean on me!"

He obeyed and we hobbled toward the car. When we arrived, Bruiser was already outside, opening the rear passenger door. Together the two of us helped the kid into the seat. Then I pushed my way to the other side and climbed in.

"What are you doing?" Kenny hollered. "Are you crazy?"

I shut the door. "That seems to be the consensus these days."

"Mikey!?"

"His leg is broken," I argued. "Urgent Care's right on the way."

"But—"

"Come on, we'll be late!"

Throwing up his hands with another oath, he turned back to the wheel and we started forward. "He's the enemy, Michael, did you ever stop to think about that?!"

I glanced at the kid who was grimacing, trying to straighten his leg.

"Here," I gently took it, allowing him to pivot in the seat so he could rest it on my lap.

"Thanks," he gasped.

"So are you?" I asked, as we pulled out of the gate and started down the highway.

"Am I what?"

"The enemy?"

He swallowed. "You mean am I working for Rushmore Pictures?"

I cocked my head at him. "Sorry?"

"The guys trying to smear you."

The car grew quiet.

"Smear me?" I repeated.

"What'd you say?" Kenny asked, looking into the mirror.

"Rushmore Pictures. They got some of the fellows on payroll. You know, to find dirt on you so they can swing the Academy votes toward their guy instead of you."

If the car was quiet before, it was a morgue now. I glanced at Kenny in the mirror. He looked as stunned as I felt.

"Didn't you know?" the kid asked. He chuckled nervously, trying to sound in-the-loop. "Shoot, I thought everybody knew that."

– – –

As good and—well, there was no other word for it but *self-righteous*— as I'd felt about putting my hate aside to help the reporter, I felt many times worse than that about my new feelings toward Rushmore Pictures. Anger and rage boiled inside of me. I'd worked hard for the recognition the Awards were offering—twenty years of sweat and hunger and sacrifice. And now some corporation was trying to take it all away. Some faceless organization that didn't even have the decency to do it honestly but used the coward's weapons of lies and rumor and innuendo!

My head spun. How deep did it go? What about Buchanan and last night's shoot-out? He'd worked for Rushmore Pictures before. Had his sudden display of "artistic temperament" been premeditated as a payment for past favors? Or maybe he had hopes of getting a new picture green-lighted over there and—I pressed my temples, trying to stop my mind from chasing itself. And what of Cassandra's appearance at the house? Why last night? Why the photographer who just happened to be parked outside? Why—

Stop it! I ordered myself. *Stop it!*

But how could I stop? It was impossible. I began thinking of retaliation. A little eye-for-an-eye. Make it clear that Michael T. Steel was not someone to mess with. And if you did, then be prepared to face his full—

STOP IT!

But I couldn't. I couldn't stop the thoughts churning and bubbling as we drove to Urgent Care. I couldn't stop them when we dropped the kid off. And I couldn't stop them when we got back onto the highway and headed for church. It's one thing to read Jesus' flowery words about not returning evil for evil, about turning the other cheek—but to actually live them when someone's coming after you, well, that's another matter—especially when your livelihood is at stake!

And so the thoughts continued spinning. Oh, every few minutes I caught myself. Every few minutes I tried to be the good Christian and push the hatred from my mind. But as soon as I pushed it out one door, it came flooding back through a dozen more. It was no good. Not only did the hatred remain, but it grew, consuming more and more of me. *Murder.* That's what Christ called this type of anger. *Murder!* Well then, like it or not, I had become a murderer. Because not only couldn't I stop, I didn't want to!

I noticed the car slowing and turning into the Zuma Beach parking lot. "Kenny? What's going on?" I asked.

"Got to make a little pickup," he said.

"What?"

He pulled the car alongside a black BMW SUV—one of a dozen in our community. But this one I recognized instantly. From its front seat emerged a pair of long legs, a trim body in a white skirt, peach jacket, and a very familiar face framed in honey-gold hair.

"Tanya?" I protested to Kenny. "What are you doing picking up my wife?"

He gave no answer and avoided my eyes in the mirror as Bruiser stepped out and opened the rear passenger door for her. She gave him a nod and slid into the seat beside me.

"Thanks for coming, Tanya," Kenny said.

"Certainly, Kenneth. Did you think I wouldn't?" Before he could respond, she turned toward me. "Mikey . . . I'm so sorry to hear what happened."

"You are?" I croaked, regretting the words before they'd left my mouth.

The slightest frown crossed her face. "Of course. Why wouldn't I be?"

I could think of a hundred reasons, but decided to swallow them. Instead, I rubbed my forehead. "Sorry," I muttered. "It's been a long night."

"I'm sorry too," she said, reaching out and patting my knee. "I'm sorry too."

I stared down at her hand, perplexed.

Kenny spoke from the front. "I asked Tanya to come with us to church. You know, to show solidarity, that kind of thing."

"Thanks," I said.

She nodded and gave a tight smile. Then, with nothing more to say, she turned to look out at the passing ocean.

— — —

I should not have been surprised at the sermon topic, or its text . . .

"Be careful not to do your 'acts of righteousness' before men, to be seen by them. If you do, you will have no reward from your Father in heaven. So when you give to the needy, do not announce it with trumpets, as the hypocrites do in the synagogues and on the streets,

to be honored by men. I tell you the truth, they have received their reward in full. But when you give to the needy, do not let your left hand know what your right hand is doing, so that your giving may be in secret. Then your Father, who sees what is done in secret, will reward you."

Now, besides my anger and hatred, here was another failure rising up and dragging me under. Here we sat, the quintessential Christian couple, posing for all to see, "practicing our righteousness" in spades. No one had to tell me we were giving new definition to the word *hypocrite*.

Pastor Barbour, healthy and tan with distinguished gray hair, went on to deliver the sermon—something about the donation box of the Old Testament Temple being made of brass so everyone could hear the clanging of coins as the devout dropped their money into it. But how different was their hollow clanging of piety from my own? The answer . . . I swallowed . . . the answer was that theirs was real. At least their piety had substance. Mine, with its failures on every front—its pride, its showmanship, its hatred, its smiling wife divorcing me—was all a sham.

I'd been told that that word, *hypocrite*, meant actor. How perfect. How pathetic. My profession had become such a part of my life that it even followed me here, into God's presence!

Pastor Barbour flipped to another section and continued reading:

"When you fast, do not look somber as the hypocrites do, for they disfigure their faces to show men they are fasting. I tell you the truth, they have received their reward in full. But when you fast, put oil on your head and wash your face, so that it will not be obvious to men that you are fasting, but only to your Father, who is unseen; and your Father, who sees what is done in secret, will reward you."

I shook my head, self-loathing growing to an all-time high. *Fasting?* I never fasted. I was too busy for such a thing. It was too inconvenient, too uncomfortable. But what had Jesus just said? *"When* you fast." Not *"if* you fast," but *"when."* In my circles, missing one meal was considered a hardship. What was Jesus talking about . . . a day, a week, a month, set aside without food, as a sacrifice for God? Amazing. Unbelievable. God was lucky if I sacrificed an hour a week to Him in a padded pew!

Who was I fooling? I couldn't live the life Christ demanded. I couldn't even come close. I was a liar. A fraud. A hypocrite.

Cursed are the rich for theirs is the kingdom of emptiness.

Cursed are the fat cats for they shall die of starvation.

Cursed is the matinee idol for he will inherit nothing.

Who did I think I was? So full of pride and arrogance and ego?

Enough!

Spoiled, self-centered.

Enough!

Full of hate and malice and lust and envy and murder!

Enough! No more! I could not live His commands. I had tried. With all of my might, I had tried. And I had failed. Any more attempts would only make me a greater hypocrite, a greater mockery to God!

It was time to quit. Time to throw in the towel before I caused any more trouble, any more embarrassment, any more shame.

I felt myself rising from the pew. Tanya looked up, her face filling with concern, no doubt fearful for our image. But I was through with images. I was through being what I was not. Let someone else try to live Christ's impossible standards. I was done faking them. I was done being schizophrenic—winner one minute, loser the next; holy Joe, filthy sinner; shining victor, shameful failure.

No more! I was done!

I stood up. "Excuse me," I whispered, motioning to the couple beside me. They pulled in their feet so I could pass. As I headed toward the aisle I could see heads turning, feel eyes following. But I didn't care. I was done caring. I was no closer to following Christ's perfection than when I'd started.

Once I made it into the aisle, I turned and quickly strode toward the back, keeping my eyes fixed on the beige carpet before me until I arrived at the heavy oak doors, pushed them open, and exited the church.

CHAPTER 6

CHAPTER 6
CHAPTER 6
CHAPTER 6
CHAPTER 6

I didn't have the courage to return to the house and battle more reporters. So Kenny agreed to swing by the place, grab some clothes and my mountain bike, and deliver them to me a mile or so up the beach at a public restroom. I needed to work out. Badly. I needed to ride long and hard. I needed to drown the anger, the betrayal, the self-accusations screaming in my head. I'd been able to hold them back a little, sometimes for minutes, but as soon as I dropped my guard, they roared back in. Like the surf they briefly retreated, then returned, thundering and crashing down upon me.

I thanked Kenny, grabbed my bike, and started to ride.

After about twenty minutes I reached Preston Beach, veered across the highway, and took the canyon trail inland. It's a tough ride, nine miles of narrow dirt and rock that wind steeply through the Santa Monica Mountains. But, like I said, I needed it.

The air was filled with sage, grass, and chaparral—smells so strong that it made my nose tickle. I sailed under a canopy of century-old oaks. Mottled light and shadow strobed into my eyes. I was glad to see the steep hills rising ahead. They were enemies to be conquered—my Rushmore Pictures, my Buchanans, my anger and rage and failure. I hit the first one like a soldier taking a ridge. And the next. And the next. Soon I was breathing hard, my heart pounding, but that was all right; it was the cost of doing battle.

I careened around a sharp corner—

"Look out!" an elderly hiker shouted.

I swerved up the bank and down again, throwing dust into the air and missing her by inches.

"Sorry!" I shouted, moving so fast that I didn't hear her response. Probably just as well.

I pumped up another hill, my thighs and calves starting to burn, until I crested and shot through a small meadow. Normally the brief respite of flat land would have been welcomed. Not today. Today it meant resting, which meant running the risk of thinking. I pushed harder, the grass and wildflowers a blur as I picked up speed for the next hill.

I hit its base and raced up . . . until two bikers appeared from nowhere, swerving to opposite sides to avoid collision.

"Sorry!" I shouted again.

Unlike the hiker's, their curses I could hear.

It was then I forced myself to pull back. I couldn't go at this intensity forever. My body couldn't take it. (Not to mention my fellow hikers and bikers.) My diversion had to be more than physical. I had to exercise some mental discipline as well. But what?

I thought of an old acting trick—one that beginners use to overcome stage fright. As a defense, we are taught to fill our minds with so many thoughts that we literally forget the audience is sitting out there staring at us. They could be the thoughts our own character would be having, thoughts about fellow characters, thoughts of just about anything. Anything except the audience.

I remembered my first day in acting class. As the new kid, my teacher made me stand in front of a dozen other students and do absolutely nothing for five, ten, fifteen minutes. I could do nothing but stand and be meticulously scrutinized. It was agony, unspeakable torture for a young, self-conscious wannabe. All I could feel were my own inadequacies, my body stiffening, my shoulders rising, my entire self becoming paralyzed with fear.

The experience was so awful that I nearly quit right then and there.

But I returned. And my reward? The instructor made me do it all over again. Only this time he threw a box of thumbtacks onto the floor and told me to pick them up. Funny, but the freedom that came from having something to do, from filling my mind with something other than myself, diverted my fear of the staring classmates.

That's what I had to do now—divert my mind, fill it with something else. And since I hadn't totally turned my back on God—on trying to follow His Sermon, yes, but not on God (I'm a fool, but not that big of one)—and since I was in a tight spot with Charlie and the press, I thought maybe praying wouldn't hurt. But not specific prayers over my problems—no, the whole idea was to forget them. Instead I wanted something a bit more generic.

At first I thought of reciting some Hail Marys or the Rosary or something. But the fact that I'm not Catholic and didn't know those prayers was a bit of a hindrance. Of course, there was the ever-popular "Now I lay me down to sleep"; or "God is great, God is good, let us thank Him for our food"; but neither felt entirely appropriate.

Then I remembered another. I'd said it a hundred times in Sunday school and church. In fact, it was even part of the Sermon on the Mount. (Not that I'd hold that against it.) In any case, it seemed fitting, so I gave it a try . . .

"Our Father who art in heaven." I spoke the words and they vibrated in my chest and mouth as I bounced down the bank of a dry rocky creek bed and up the other side. But I didn't want to simply recite them. I didn't want to turn them into some mindless chant. After all, words are important, particularly to actors. So I forced myself to think over each phrase, chewing it, meditating upon it:

Our Father who art in heaven . . .

I've never been big on fathers, especially having had a dad who considered beating his kids part of his daily devotions. But I could tell where Jesus was going with this. He didn't say "Our God" or "Our Lord" but . . . "Our *Father.*" Interesting. No other religion I could think of talked about having this type of relationship with God. This God was not the personless "force" that the Eastern mystics describe. Nor the Allah of absolute justice that the Muslims teach. Not even the Jewish *Yahweh*, so terrifyingly holy that His name was forbidden from being spoken out loud.

No. This was *Father* . . . as in a personal, caring parent.

More than that, it was *Our* Father—as in we're all in this together.

But Jesus didn't stop there. He continued with our Father who is *"in heaven."* Interesting balance. Even though God is a caring, loving parent, He's still in heaven, He's still God overseeing everything from His throne. What extreme opposites . . .

Supreme Deity. Caring parent.

I hit a flat stretch of ground and shifted to a higher gear, picking up speed. I began chewing on the next set of words. Just in case we think this Fatherhood somehow diminishes God's holiness, that we can stroll on up to Him, all casual and informal, Jesus continues with . . .

. . . hallowed be Your name.

Although I'd recited the prayer since I was a kid, I'd never really stopped to consider this angle. How interesting that the very first thing Jesus does (once He's established who we're praying to) is to worship Him, to declare His holiness. I shook my head in mild amusement. How different this was from my own prayers, which usually start off with me whining, then lead to my shopping list of requests, then end in a grand finale of more whining (just to make sure He got the point).

But this approach was entirely different. It put the focus on *God*, on what *He* should receive.

I started up another hill. It was loose with dirt and so steep that I dropped into one of the lowest gears. I was pushing again; I couldn't help myself. I thought about the next phrase:

Your kingdom come, Your will be done . . .

Amazing . . . the prayer *still* focused upon God, upon *His* agenda, upon *His* will. And this business of *Your kingdom?* Surely He was talking about the same kingdom He'd mentioned earlier, the same "kingdom of heaven."

The path grew steeper. I dropped all the way down to first. I stood up, pumping hard, inching my way up, my legs aching, my heart hammering.

Your kingdom come, Your will be done on earth as it is in heaven.

On earth? *On earth?* He wasn't just talking about His kingdom being up in heaven. He was talking about bringing it down here to earth!

But how?

I tried to block the answer, but it surfaced. Since the kingdom wasn't here physically, at least not yet, its principles were to be lived in this earthly kingdom by . . . I took a gulp of air . . . by the *inhabitants* of His heavenly kingdom. And since I doubted He was talking about angels coming down to set up housekeeping, that left . . . I took another breath . . . that left *me.* People like *me.* After all, wasn't I already a citizen of heaven? I didn't become a citizen just when I died. I had become one back when I first accepted Christ, when I had first accepted His . . . kingship. And, as a subject of the King, as a citizen of His kingdom, I was expected to live by His kingdom's rules. That's how His kingdom came (at least for now), through people like me, through its citizens, by living in this earthly kingdom but following the principles of His heavenly kingdom.

But I couldn't! I'd just proven it! No matter how I tried, I failed! I could not live by His rules!

My eyes began to burn. I blinked back the tears and pressed on, pedaling harder, faster, trying once again to drown out my thoughts.

Give us today our daily bread.

Good. Here was something I could deal with. Deal with because it wasn't a concern. What did I need daily bread for? I didn't. Not with my bank accounts, my stock portfolio, my real estate. This one I had nailed. I didn't need to deal with it.

Or did I?

Again my brain churned. Wasn't there another type of bread? Wasn't it Christ, Himself, who said He was the *"Bread of Life"*? Granted, maybe literal food wasn't a concern for me, maybe I had all I needed. But what of spiritual food? Just as I couldn't go a day without eating physical food, what made me think I could go without eating spiritual food, without His presence feeding my soul . . . feeding it *daily*?

But how? How? *How?* How could His presence be my food, my sustenance, when He made such impossible demands?!

I started up a series of steep switchbacks, my legs growing numb, my breath cutting a groove into the back of my throat.

Forgive us our debts, as we also have forgiven our debtors.

The clarity struck so hard that I nearly missed a corner, bouncing over exposed roots, catching air, then hitting the edge of the path and continuing on.

How many times had I prayed this prayer? A hundred? A thousand? But what was I really saying? Had I really been asking God to forgive me only *as I forgive others?* To forgive me only to the degree that I forgave?! And to have prayed that prayer over and over again? Would He really forgive me only as I forgave Buchanan? Only as I forgave Rushmore Pictures? Only as I forgave the reporters and whoever else was intent on destroying me?

My legs had lost feeling. My side cramped. I crested the hill but continued pushing. Harder. Faster. I had no choice. I was zooming. Flying.

And lead us not into temptation, but deliver us from the evil one.

Temptation!? Everywhere I looked I was being tempted! And everywhere I was losing! There was no hope of winning. Not this race! Not these demands! Not with my pride and anger and hatred and hypocrisy and unforgiveness and—

"WATCH IT!"

I looked up to see a father and his little girl. They had no time to move and I couldn't miss them—not without dumping the bike. It was either them or the bushes. Instinctively I chose the bushes. I heard the girl scream as I veered away and sailed over an unseen ledge. I hadn't seen the ledge, but I now saw my future—a huge patch of poison oak just below. My front wheel slammed into the ground and I flew over the handlebars, twisting and tumbling in the air. I hit hard, bouncing once, twice, before rolling, rolling, rolling through the endless clumps of shiny, three-leaf plants, praying that I'd come to a stop.

Eventually my prayer was answered. Unfortunately it was by a large and rather unyielding eucalyptus tree.

– – –

The line of cars and vans parked outside my fence started a hundred yards from the gate. Fortunately, no one recognized the bedraggled biker with helmet and shades who limped past them, pushing his twisted bike with the bent wheel. Some were dozing, others reading the Sunday *Times*. One even had his door open and was listening to an all-too-familiar radio evangelist who, you guessed it, had started up right where I'd left off:

> *"For if you forgive men when they sin against you, your heavenly Father will also forgive you-a. But if you do not forgive men their sins, your Father will not forgive your sins."*

To be forgiven only as we forgive. The concept must have been important to Jesus for Him to go back and repeat it in the Sermon. I took a deep, purging breath and let it out. Once again I got the point. And once again I realized the futility of obeying it.

I approached the security box at the gate as discretely as possible. Quickly I entered my code. I was covered with poison oak, head to toe, and was in a hurry to soap up and wash off the oil before the reactions began.

"Michael!" A nearby reporter spotted me and leaped into action.

Others followed. "Michael! Mr. Steel!" They quickly surrounded me as the gate swung open.

"Guys," I warned, "I'm covered in—"

"Mr. Steel, tell me, what will this do to your chances for the Oscar?"

They crowded against my bike, my clothes, against every area that had been exposed to the poison oak oil. Again I tried to warn them. "Guys, I'm completely covered in—"

"Have criminal charges been filed?"

"Have you given any thought to—"

"Guys!"

But they refused to listen. So, shrugging and trying not to laugh, I moved forward as they pushed and crowded against me.

"Mr. Steel," another shouted. "Would you mind telling us what's so funny?"

I merely shook my head.

"Mr. Steel, this is no laughing matter!" It was a young reporter, cocky and bold. He'd peeled off his shirt to catch a few rays and hadn't bothered to put it back on. "I mean, do you honestly find being a pedophile that amusing?"

I slowed to a stop and looked at him.

The group quieted. He did not budge. He did not flinch.

Finally I spoke. "What's your name, son?"

"Brent Parker." He held his ground, indignant and dripping with self-righteousness.

Slowly I reached out my hand to him. He looked at it, puzzled, then took it. We shook firmly as I held his hand with both of mine. Then I pulled him into an embrace, wrapping my arms about his bare shoulders and back, pressing my chest against his.

When I finished, I turned and headed up the driveway.

Caught off guard for only a moment, the youth regained his indignation. "You still didn't answer the question!"

I continued up the drive toward my front door.

"Mr. Steel, what on earth do you see that's so amusing?"

I didn't bother to answer. I figured he'd find out in just a few hours. They'd all find out when the poison oak kicked in. God forgive me, but if I was going to fail at forgiving others, then at least I would enjoy it.

CHAPTER 7

CHAPTER 7
CHAPTER 7
CHAPTER 7
CHAPTER 7

"You're a moron, Toad."

"Tell me about it," I mumbled, trying to see out the van's window. I would have succeeded if my eyes hadn't been swollen shut. I turned back to Annie, speaking to her blurry form behind the wheel. "When I got home, I lathered up with soap. Twice! Every inch of my body— inside my ears, my nose, you name it, I washed it."

"And you thought you wouldn't need medication? After you'd been exposed for what, two hours?"

"Almost three," I muttered, rubbing my arm.

"Stop scratching," she ordered. She took a sip of decaf tea from her mug. This always made me nervous as she had a habit of closing her eyes whenever she drank. No problem when she was behind a table or a counter. A bit nerve-racking when she was behind the wheel. She finished her drink and repeated, "Total moron."

I wish I could disagree, but I couldn't. It was true. I had showered thoroughly. I had thought I'd scrubbed off the poison. But two-and-a-half hours was more than enough time for the oil to soak into my skin and start an allergic reaction. I didn't know it right after the shower, but I knew it ten hours later when I woke up in bed with my arms, legs, and face on fire. My skin was literally crawling, itching beyond belief. I had thrown off the covers and staggered into the bathroom. Snapping on the light, I looked into the mirror. Some swollen-faced monster from the Outer Limits stared back at me.

I had to visit a doctor.

But since I could barely see to walk, let alone drive, I had given Kenny a call. Unfortunately, Kenny had the good sense not to pick up.

I then hobbled toward the balcony, touching and rubbing dozens of different patches on my body along the way. I knew better than to scratch. I didn't have to. Just the touching brought unspeakable relief. But as soon as I had completed the circuit, touching my last rash, the first had flared back up. From the balcony I squinted through puffy eyes, looking for my media pals. Apparently my little "meet and greet" with them yesterday afternoon had done some good. There were only a handful of vehicles in sight.

Which meant it would be safe to call Annie.

It was 3:10 when she arrived in her beater panel truck.

It was now 3:18 as we cruised down the road and she reached over to turn on the radio.

"Do not store up for yourselves treasures on earth, where moth and rust destroy, and where thieves break in and stee-yul."

"Oh, no," I groaned, "don't tell me you're listening to him too?"

"No." She sounded perplexed. "I've never heard this guy. Who is he?"

"He seems to be on every radio and TV station in town."

"But I was listening to classical." She reached over and started changing channels. I almost told her not to bother, but figured she'd find out soon enough. As I expected, all she got was static . . . until she returned to the same channel and we heard:

"But store up for yourselves treasures in heaven, where moth and rust do not destroy, and where thieves do not break in and stee-yul."

Of course it was the Sermon on the Mount. And while Annie was irritated, I was almost amused. No matter what I did there was no getting away from it. Or its truths.

"For where your treasure is, there your heart will be also."

I shook my head. How perfectly that thought described the two of us. Me, who had all the treasures a person could imagine; and Annie, who didn't even have a savings account. What's the old saying, "The rich are not those who have the most, but those who need the least"? If that was the case, then Annie was the richest person I knew. Her treasure had always been in people. Her investment always in their lives . . . pouring herself into pimps, hookers, runaways, and crazies—driving all the way to Malibu to help her little brother at 3:00 in the morning. That's where her wealth lay—in people, in their souls. And her reward? For those who invest money, they receive money. For those like Annie who invest in life . . . they receive life.

And my return?

In just thirty-six hours some thief had broken in and was stealing everything. All my work and sacrifice was disappearing before my eyes.

I glanced back at Annie, who was finishing off her lukewarm tea. Sure, she had her setbacks, her heartbreaks—but moth and rust and thieves would never touch her investments.

"The eye is the lamp of the body. If your eyes are good, your whole body will be full of light. But if your eyes are bad, your whole body will be full of darkness. If then the light within you is darkness, how great is that darkness!"

I dropped down the visor and checked myself in the vanity mirror. Eyes? I couldn't even see my eyes. Who knew what was in them? Especially now.

I motioned to the radio. "Do we need to listen to that?"

"Nope." She reached over and turned it off.

Ah, blessed silence.

Too bad it wouldn't last.

— — —

Urgent Care was open and booming with business. Seems there was an outbreak of poison oak—especially among some of my buddies in the media.

"Hey, guys," I said, recognizing a voice or two as we entered and Annie signed me in. "What's up?"

"Steel, is that you?" An older guy from Channel 2 asked.

"What happened?" some youngster croaked. "You look terrible."

I shrugged. "Just a little run-in with some poison oak. What about you guys?"

"Poison oak . . . ?"

There was a moment of silence. Then realization.

"It was *you?*" the youngster asked.

"*You're* the one?" Channel 2 demanded.

Their anger quickly grew. "Are you telling us that—"

"Mr. Steel?" The receptionist stood in the open door. "The doctor will see you now." Whether she was playing celebrity favorites or knew I needed to be rescued, I didn't know. I was just glad to get out of the room. Even as the door closed and we moved down the hall I heard their voices.

"Oh, man, it *was* him."

"He'll get his!"

"That's right, what goes around, comes around!"

I smiled. The way I figured, the *come around* part, at least for them, had already arrived.

After a brief examination by the doctor followed by a hefty cortisone shot in the rear, I was given steroid pills with a schedule like a NASA countdown—seven pills for day one, six for day two, five for day three, etc. Next came the quick and unpleasant duty of calling Robert Meisner, my producer. It looked like I'd have to be off the shoot for the next several days.

It took six rings to rouse him, but as soon as he heard my voice he was wide awake. By the time I told him my dilemma, he was shouting. "Long sleeves!" he exclaimed. "We'll cover your arms in long sleeves!"

"It's all over my face."

"But . . . but . . . makeup, we'll cover you in makeup!"

I turned and asked the doctor, who shook his head, saying it would only make things worse.

"Okay, okay." Robert was growing more desperate, no doubt out of bed and pacing. "Then long shots! We'll shoot you from a distance!"

"It'll have to be from Cleveland. I look like a leper."

"Great! A rewrite! Yes, a massive rewrite where you visit a leper colony in India and contract—"

"Robert—"

"But . . ."

"It'll only be a few days."

"But . . . but . . ."

"A week, max."

"But . . . but . . . but . . ." The poor guy was sputtering like a motorboat. Not that I blamed him. With each "but" he was no doubt calculating the hundreds of thousands of dollars going down the drain.

— — —

After saying good-bye to the doctor (and my press pals) Annie and I headed outside to her van. Her limp seemed more painful, and when I mentioned it, she simply chalked it up to the damp, predawn fog, then changed topics. "Listen, I have an idea," she said. "Why don't you think about staying with me for the next few days?"

"What?"

"Sure, until this thing with the poison oak and Charlie blows over."

"As what," I chuckled, "one of your halfway residents?"

"Why not?"

"I'm not exactly sure I qualify as being in a halfway crisis."

She shrugged. "I don't know anyone who's more halfway than you."

"What's that supposed to mean?"

She stared down at the asphalt as we continued walking. The fog seemed to enclose the sound of our footsteps.

"Annie?"

She said nothing.

"What's that supposed to mean?"

Finally she looked up, then quietly quoted:

"No one can serve two masters. Either he will hate the one and love the other, or he will be devoted to the one and despise the other. You cannot serve both God and Money."

Gravel scraped under my shoes as I stopped. "That's the Sermon on the Mount!"

"Yes, it is," she said. She didn't slow but continued limping toward the van. "And that, little brother, has been your whole problem."

I stared for a moment, not sure I understood. Then I moved to catch up.

She continued. "You're caught halfway between two worlds, and it's tearing you apart. On the one hand, you want to succeed with this Sermon on the Mount, this kingdom of God you keep talking about. On the other, you want the fame, power, and money of our world."

"You're talking like it's *either/or*," I argued. "Like you can't pursue both."

She crossed to my side of the van to unlock the door and quietly repeated:

"Either he will hate the one and love the other, or he will be devoted to the one and despise the other."

My mood soured. Between my crawling skin and Annie's unsolicited sermon, I was anything but patient. "So what am I supposed to do?" I demanded. "Sell everything, quit my job, and become a monk?"

"I don't think you could stand the haircut." She turned back to me. "It's not what you *do*, Toad. It's who you *are*."

Anger rose, tightening my jaw, as she moved around to unlock her side. "You don't think I'm trying to change?" I fought to keep my voice even. "What do you think all of this is about? It's about me trying to change, Annie, it's about me trying to be different!"

"And that's why you're failing." She opened her door and crawled in behind the wheel.

"What?" She said nothing as I slipped into my seat. "What's that supposed to mean?"

"It means you'll succeed for a while. In one area or another. But it's like pitching a tent in a hurricane. As soon as you get one corner staked down another two fly up. Then you get them secure and the first one flies back up—and on and on you go, chasing your tail 'til you're exhausted." She pushed the hair from her eyes. "And from what I've seen, little brother, that's about where you are now."

I wanted to say something, anything, but no words came. She'd nailed me, perfectly, as only one sibling can nail another. She'd completely managed to sum up my life for the past week. Yes, sometimes I'd win—as the peacemaker in the dressing room trailer, as salt and light on the set, as Mr. Chaste in the entry hall with Cassandra. But, just when I was feeling self-confident, I'd meet defeat—my anger toward Buchanan, my hatred toward Rushmore Pictures, my unforgiveness toward the press. Back and forth I went like some spiritual Ping-Pong ball, winning and losing, losing and winning, one moment Christ's greatest follower, the next His greatest hypocrite.

Annie closed her door and turned on the ignition. Immediately, the radio blared on.

"Therefore I tell you, do not worry about your life, what you will eat or drink; or about your body, what you will way-ur. Is not life more important than food, and the body more important than clothes?"

I groaned. "Unbelievable . . ."

Annie reached over to turn it off. But instead of off, she actually managed to turn it louder. Then, louder some more.

"Look at the birds of the air; they do not sow or reap or store away in barns, and yet your heavenly Father feeds them. Are you not much more valuable than they?"

"Turn it off," I shouted.

"I'm trying," she yelled.

"Who of you by worrying can add a single hour to his life?"

She continued twisting the knob, the words blasting even louder. "It won't turn off!" she shouted. "It's jammed!"

"And why do you worry about clothes?"

I reached over and tried. She was right—the knob was turned all the way up and frozen solid.

"See how the lilies of the field grow. They do not labor or spin."

"Change the channel!" I yelled, still fighting the volume knob. "Change the stupid channel!"

"Yet I tell you that not even Solomon in all his splendor was dressed like one of thee-yuz."

She began pressing buttons, one after another, but the little red needle did not move.

"If that is how God clothes the grass of the field, which is here today and tomorrow is thrown into the fire, will he not much more clothe you, O you of little faith?"

I reached for the channel selector knob. It turned freely but the needle remained fixed.

"So do not worry, saying, 'What shall we eat?' or 'What shall we drink?' or 'What shall we way-ur?'"

I slammed the radio with my fist. Nothing. I slammed it again. Then again.
"Mikey!"
I hit it again, my anger and rage growing and consuming.
And still it continued.
And still I pounded.

"For the pagans run after all these things, and your heavenly Father knows that you need them."

I spotted Annie's empty mug on the dash and grabbed it.
"Michael!"

"But seek first his kingdom and his righteousness, and all these things will be given to you as well."

I smashed it into the radio. Annie screamed as pieces exploded and flew.
And still it continued.
I hit it again. Then again, the handle breaking off, cutting into my palm as I kept smashing.
"Mikey!"

"Therefore do not worry about tomorrow, for tomorrow will worry about itself. Each day has enough trouble of its own."

Finally, I shattered the face of the radio. There was a surge of sparks, a slight crackle, then silence. Except for my heavy, uneven breathing, nothing but silence.

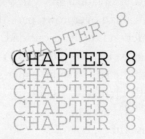

CHAPTER 8

We rode in silence the rest of the way to Jeremiah's Place. Not a word—just Annie's quiet understanding that I needed solitude, and my own grudging, sulking broodiness. It wasn't until she pulled into the driveway, turned off the ignition, and sat with me in the morning stillness that I spoke.

"So how do I do it?"

"Do what?" she asked.

"Nail down all those tent pegs. Live the Sermon on the Mount."

"Are you really sure that's what you—"

"Of course I am," I snapped. Then, a little softer, "Yes, I'm sure."

"It's not something you just jump into."

I nodded, muttering, "Tell me about it."

She took a breath. "All right, then . . . the first thing you need to know is—" She hesitated, unsure how to begin.

"Is what?" I asked.

"Is that you can't."

"You're making me crazy!"

She looked at me with that lopsided grin of hers. "Sorry." Then, glancing at her watch, she added, "We've still got an hour before the house wakes up. Can I show you something?"

"Please. Anything."

She reached for the ignition, turned it back on, and we pulled into the street.

– – –

Minutes later we were traipsing up a grassy dew-covered hill that overlooked the city. It was a small overgrown park that we used to play in as kids . . . or hide in, depending upon our dad's temperament. What had once been saplings were now tall trees. Young pink-and-white oleanders had grown to the size of small garages.

"The place has really changed," I said.

"You never visit it?" she asked.

"I've driven by a few times, but . . ."

She nodded, seeming to understand. "Follow me."

We made our way around a peninsula of brush and trees until we arrived at a nearly hidden path. Annie pushed aside the branches, and I followed, trying to avoid their whipping into my face. At last we entered a small clearing. It was about twenty yards in diameter. Near the center stood a well-pruned fruit tree, twelve, maybe fourteen feet high. Annie motioned to it and proudly asked, "So what do you think?"

I stared, not entirely sure what I was looking at. "A tree," I ventured. "It's an apple tree."

"Exactly." She stepped closer, surveying it. "I planted it a couple years after Dad died."

I felt myself stiffen slightly. "Why?"

She paused a moment. Then, brushing a curl from her face, she answered. "Because I'd finally gotten a clue on how to forgive him."

I coughed, nearly choking. "Forgive him! After what he did to us? To you!"

She said nothing, though I saw her hand drop self-consciously to her crippled hip.

I shook my head—not only at the idea of forgiveness, but at the impossibility of it—at least for me. Then again, if one was really serious about the Sermon, I suppose even forgiving monsters like my father was important. And, if that was the case, well, you could add another failure to my list.

I turned to her and quietly quoted, "'Forgive us our debts, as we forgive our debtors.'"

"That's what it says."

I felt my throat tighten. I wasn't sure why—anger, guilt, frustration, all of the above? When I spoke, my voice was so husky words barely came. "How?" I cleared my throat and tried again. "How did you do it?"

"That was the easy part."

"*Easy?*"

She turned back to the tree. "You see those buds on the branches?" I looked and nodded.

"In a few months, they'll be full-grown apples."

"I understand how fruit grows, Annie."

She turned to me, then shrugged. "Maybe you do, maybe you don't. Listen . . ." She cocked her head. "Do you hear that?"

"Hear what?"

"From the branches."

I frowned, hearing nothing but birds and the distant spitting of an automatic sprinkler.

"Can't you hear that?" she asked. "The way they're grunting and groaning, the way they're straining to grow apples?"

I looked at her and answered flatly, "No."

She smiled. "Neither do I. But isn't that exactly what you're trying to do? Aren't you out there grunting and groaning and straining to grow your own fruit, trying to follow all the rules and regulations of the Sermon on your own?"

"Who else is going to do it for me?"

"Who does it for these branches?"

"Nobody. It just happens naturally."

"How?"

"What do you mean, 'how?' The sap flows through the trunk and into the branches. They don't do anything."

She shook her head. "That's not true. Those branches have to do something."

I waited.

"They have to stay attached to the tree." She looked back at it. "What was it Christ said about Him being the trunk and you and me being the branches? '*If a man remains in me and I in him, he can bear much fruit; but apart from me you can do nothing.*'" She turned back to me. "You cannot live Christ's commands, Toad. No matter how hard you try, you'll fail. I think you've pretty well proven that by now, don't you?"

I looked down at the ground, scowling.

She continued, softer. "The key isn't in your trying, it's in your connectedness."

"What are you talking about?" I muttered. "I believe in Christ."

When she didn't answer, I looked up. There was that grin again. Finally she spoke. "So do the demons, Toad. According to the Bible, they believe too."

My scowl deepened. I had no idea where she was going.

"But believing in Him . . . and letting His love control you. Those are two different things."

"*Control me?*" I asked.

She looked back at the tree. "I couldn't forgive Daddy. I tried, believe me. I tried everything I knew. But nothing worked. It was only when I took my eyes off the fruit that I was trying to bear and focused on the Lord, upon my relationship with Him—only then did the fruit appear. And it appeared as naturally and effortlessly as these apples are appearing."

"I believe in Christ!" I repeated. "I try to follow His teachings, I try not to break His commands."

"It's not about breaking His commands, Toad. It's about breaking His heart."

The words cut deep. I closed my eyes. Why was she talking to me like I wasn't a Christian? I'd received Christ as a child. We both had. Together we did the Sunday school thing, the church thing. We'd been Christians our entire lives. But this . . . I coughed again, trying to hide my irritation. "So what am I supposed to do, just sit around and wait to feel warm fuzzies toward Him? Is that what you're talking about?"

She didn't answer.

"We've got to do something!" I insisted. "We just can't sit around and examine our navels!"

"Yes." She turned back to the tree. "We have to do something. We have to stay connected. We have to let ourselves fall more deeply in love with Him. He'll do the rest."

I was anything but convinced. "What about you?" I demanded.

"What about me?"

"You're not just sitting around, all doe-eyed and loving. You're always out there doing things ... at Jeremiah's Place ... for me, for others. You're *always* doing."

She shook her head. "No. That's not me. The doing comes from Him. From His love. And when I get sick and tired of the people at the house, or of your whining, or of my own stubborn selfishness—I don't suck it up and try to do better." She turned back to the tree. "I look to Christ and He makes me better."

"We have to take *some* responsibility," I argued.

"Yes and no. What did we hear down at Urgent Care on the radio?"

"I was a little preoccupied," I mumbled.

"'*Seek first his kingdom and his righteousness, and all these things will be given to you.*' Christ wasn't just talking about things like clothes and food, little brother. He was talking about life. As you seek Him, He'll give you the ability to live life. *His* life. *His* way."

My eyes started to burn. "But all these mess-ups," I whispered hoarsely. "My constant failings—"

"Will gradually disappear," she answered. "The more you fall in love with Christ and the more you allow His love to consume you, the more easily you'll be able to walk over those failures."

I swallowed back the tightness clawing at my throat.

"It's like Peter walking on the water. Remember, when he kept his eyes focused on Jesus, how he walked over the waves? It was only when he looked down at the water, when he took his eyes off Jesus and looked at his problems, that he sank."

I gave my eyes a discreet wipe.

Her voice grew more gentle. "And that's what you've been doing, Toad. Looking down at the water, looking for the fruit—instead of your Lord."

– – –

We'd barely pulled back into the driveway of Jeremiah's Place before the bottle blonde I'd met in Annie's office came racing toward us shouting, "Annie . . . Annie! It's Rachel, she's got a knife! She's going to kill herself!"

Immediately Annie was out of the van, limping for the house, demanding a rundown on events. I raced to her side.

"It's her lover," the blonde explained. "She called again. Said she was breaking up with her."

"At seven o'clock in the morning!"

"She'd been speeding, strung out all week."

"So she calls Rachel to spread the joy," Annie scorned. "Wonderful."

We arrived, threw open the door, and entered. Three or four of the residents stood around the perimeter of the living room, watching. Another handful viewed the scene from the stairs. Off in one corner, a scrawny teen in cutoffs and a halter top was using a serrated bread knife to hold back the big bald guy I'd met earlier. Her ebony skin glistened in sweat . . . except for her left arm where she'd opened a vein. It was covered in dark, shiny blood that dripped off her fingertips to the wood floor below.

"Rachel!" Annie cried.

The girl swung the knife around to Annie—crouching, making it clear she meant business. "Stay back!"

Annie slowed, but didn't stop. "What's going on?"

"STAY BACK!"

Glancing at Big Bald, Annie asked. "What's she on?"

He shook his head. "It's Rachel. She don't have to be on nothin'. Cecilia, her lover, called and—"

"I heard." Annie turned back to the girl. "Rachel, honey . . ."

"STAY BACK!" She lunged with the knife as a warning. "I'LL TAKE YOU WITH ME! I SWEAR TO GOD, ANNIE, I'LL TAKE YOU, TOO!"

Annie came to a stop. "What did you do to your arm, hon?"

Rachel looked down at her bloody arm and gave a slight shudder at what she saw.

"I caught her in the bathroom," the blonde explained.

Raising her bleeding arm, staring at it in contempt, Rachel sneered. "Ceci's right—I can't do nothin' right."

"I don't know, darlin'," Annie said. "Looks like you got a pretty good start there." Again she moved toward her.

And again Rachel brandished the knife. "STAY AWAY!"

Annie hesitated but continued. "Come on, Rach, it's me."

"Annie?" Big Bald warned.

She threw him a glance.

"She's HIV."

Annie nodded and turned back to her. "Let me see what you've done there, sweetheart."

I watched from the side, wanting to help, but not knowing how. I stood paralyzed, as if viewing a movie. But this was no movie. No second or third takes to get it right. This was reality. Annie's reality.

The girl had started to shiver. It may have been shock, I couldn't tell. Giant tears welled up in her eyes.

"Come on, Rach . . . ," Annie half-whispered.

"NO!" she cried, the tears spilling onto her cheeks. "NO!"

"Sweetheart—"

The girl swiped at them with her bleeding hand, smearing blood across her face and cheeks.

"Rach—"

She shook harder and pleaded. "Don't make me hurt you!" Again she wiped her face. Again she looked at her arm, this time staring at it like it belonged to someone else.

"Rachel."

"NO!" She lunged with the knife, forcing Annie to stagger backwards, the blood-coated blade missing her by inches. Big Bald and I both started forward, but Annie motioned for us to stop.

Tears streamed down the young girl's face. Her body shook as mucus dripped from her nose. She wiped it with her hand, smearing more blood. She sniffed hard, but it did no good. It continued running and dripping.

"Let me help you, sweetheart."

Trying to swallow back the tears, Rachel let out one sob and then another—gut wrenching, full of anger and pain.

"Rachel, please." Annie inched closer. "You're not in this alone. We can help."

The girl wilted ever so slightly.

Annie took the cue and closed the distance.

"Annie," Big Bald warned.

She paid no attention. "Rachel? Sweetheart?" Slowly, she reached out her hand. "Let me have the knife, okay?"

Rachel looked up, blinking, then stared at Annie's outstretched palm.

"Okay, honey?"

She looked back to the knife.

"Rachel . . ."

"I don't want to hurt you," she whimpered. "Please don't make me hurt you."

"You won't hurt me, baby."

Big Bald shifted, preparing to attack from the side, but Annie cut him a glance, another order to stay back.

"Please . . . ," the girl begged. "Please . . ."

"Just let me have the knife, sweetheart . . ."

"I don't want to—"

"I know you don't, hon, just give me the knife."

They were two feet apart.

Again the girl looked at Annie's outstretched hand. Then to the knife. She continued melting, softening.

At last, Annie stretched out both arms. "That's it, sweetheart," she said, reaching out to embrace her. "You don't want to hurt any—"

"NOOO!" Rachel leaped back and raised the knife above her head. Then, with both hands, she plunged it toward her stomach. But Annie was already moving in. She yanked the girl's arms at the bottom of the swing, barely stopping the knife from entering.

"LET ME GO!" Rachel shrieked. "LET ME GO!"

Annie hung on as the momentum threw them both to the floor. They tumbled, Annie on top, then Rachel, arms and legs flailing, blood flying.

Big Bald leaped into the fray. I followed.

Again Annie was on top, trying to pry the knife from Rachel's hands, doing her best to avoid its sharp, bloody edge. No sweet-talking now—just brutal force as Annie gripped the girl's wrists and slammed them hard onto the floor once, twice, three times before her grip broke and the knife clattered to the wood.

I kicked it away as Big Bald tried to separate them. But Annie would not have it. Instead, she wrapped her arms around the blood-covered girl. "It's okay," she whispered fiercely through her own tears. "It's okay, it's okay . . ."

Rachel fell into the hug, weeping uncontrollably.

"It's okay . . . you're all right . . . it's okay . . ."

Big Bald and I stood, unsure what to do.

How long they held each other like that, I don't know. But eventually they pulled back and looked at one another. More tears as they embraced again. When they separated, Annie reached out to wipe Rachel's blood-smeared hair from her face, then bent forward and lightly kissed her on the forehead.

Big Bald finally moved in and helped Rachel to her feet, leading her toward the kitchen, calling for a basin and washcloth, ordering someone to phone 911.

I knelt down to Annie who, by now, was nearly as bloody as Rachel.

"Are you okay?" I asked.

"Sure," she flashed me her lopsided grin. "No problem. Just your typical—" That's when she winced in pain and looked down at her side. Her shirt had been slashed and it was wet with blood. Sliding her hand under the material and gently testing her side, she grimaced. "Well, we might have a *little* problem . . ."

CHAPTER 9

"Do not judge, or you too will be judged. For in the same way you judge others, you will be judged, and with the measure you use, it will be measured to you. Why do you look at the speck of sawdust in your brother's eye and pay no attention to the plank in your own eye? How can you say to your brother, 'Let me take the speck out of your eye,' when all the time there is a plank in your own eye? You hypocrite, first take the plank out of your own eye, and then you will see clearly to remove the speck from your brother's eye."

I closed the Bible and set it on the wobbly night table in my new room—the one I shared with a junkie and a male prostitute. Not exactly the company I'm used to keeping, but it didn't bother me much. As a temporary resident, I'd made a specific point not to carry any type of superiority chip on my shoulder. I'd been friendly and courteous, treating them both like my equals. No judging here; we were one in the family of man.

Or so I thought . . . until the little confrontation in Annie's sweatbox of an office two hours earlier. It may have been two hours earlier, but as I lay on the bed, I was stinging and smarting as if it had just happened . . .

We'd returned from the E.R. by ten that morning. Rachel's arm was serious but not critical. She'd been admitted into the psychiatric ward for observation and would probably return to us within a week or so. And the wound in Annie's side? Superficial. That was the good news. The bad news was the HIV she had been exposed to through Rachel's blood.

"Why?!" I'd demanded as I paced back and forth in front of her desk.

Annie's response had been maddeningly calm as she flipped through her paperwork for the day. "Rachel was going to kill herself."

"She could have killed you!"

"That's doubtful."

"That's possible!"

She shrugged. "And your point . . . ?"

"My point! MY POINT?!" She glanced up and I lowered my voice. "My point is you risked your life for a total stranger."

"Not exactly."

"Yes, Annie, *exactly*."

"Michael," she removed her glasses, rubbing her eyes. "Let me ask you a question. Would you have done it for me—risked your life to save mine?"

"In a heartbeat. You know that."

"Why?"

"*Why?* Because you're my sister; because I love you."

"Precisely. And that's why I did it for Rachel. Because she's my sister; because I love her."

"Please . . ."

"What?"

"You're not being realistic!"

"And you're living in the wrong world again."

"What's that supposed to mean?"

"It means, like everyone else, you're quick to pay lip service about how we're all equal in the eyes of God."

"We are."

"Of course we are. Except . . ."

"Except what?"

"Except you don't believe it."

"Of course I—"

"No," she shook her head. "You say it, you act like it, but you don't believe it."

"You're telling me I'm a hypocrite?"

"I'm telling you that you've already prejudged Rachel."

"*Prejudged?*"

"Yes, prejudged, as in *prejudice*."

I felt my face flush. "How can you say that?"

"Because it's true. You've already judged her as some black lesbian kid riddled with dope and disease who'll never amount to anything and certainly isn't equal to me."

"She's *not* equal to you! Not a hundred of her!"

"In whose eyes, little brother?"

"In mine and . . . and . . ."

"And the world's?"

I swallowed, sensing a trap.

"Why do you think that is?" she asked.

"Why? Because, I mean, look at you! Look at her!"

"Because I'm running some halfway house and helping others—and she's just some street kid fighting to find herself?"

"For starters, yes."

"And you don't call that judging?"

"I call it truth."

"In your eyes, yes. But who made you judge? How do you know that five, ten, fifteen, years from now she won't be doing greater things than me?"

"Because . . . because—"

"Because she's some black lesbian kid riddled with dope and disease."

I stood staring at her, trying to find the words. "Annie," my voice thickened. "You're . . . my sister."

"Yes. And I'm grateful for it. You love me because I'm your sister. And I love you because you're my brother. That's terrific."

"It is."

"Yes. And I love *her* because *she's* my sister."

I searched her eyes, looking for any signs of falseness, any lack of resolve. There was none. "You really mean that, don't you?"

She nodded.

"But how . . . how can one person have that much love . . . for a stranger?"

"Because I quit judging her."

"Yes," my voice grew huskier, "but . . . *how?*"

It was her turn to search my eyes. When she was certain of my sincerity, she answered. "In the beginning, I couldn't. They were just people that I helped so I'd feel better about myself—products that I processed and moved through the system. But then . . . things started to change."

I looked at her, waiting for more.

"Day by day, as I grew more connected to Christ, I started seeing them through *His* eyes. Gradually, week by week, my judging faded until it was replaced by His love. A love that came as naturally as, as . . ."

" . . . as a tree bears fruit?"

"Yes," she answered softly. "It's just another type of fruit, Toad. Another fruit that you'll never be able to grow on your own."

"Mr. Steel?"

I looked up from my bed, startled from the memories of our conversation. Big Bald was now standing in the doorway to my room. "There's something on TV Annie wants you to see."

"What is it?" I asked, rising.

"It's . . . uh . . . You better come see it."

Moments later, I was back in Annie's office staring at an old twelve-inch black-and-white TV that sat on a sagging bookshelf. Mandy Wright from *Entertainment Today* was on the screen, shoving a microphone into the face of director Colin Buchanan. In the background was Sound Stage 11, the bedroom set of *The Devil's Breath.*

"I'm uncertain of the details," Buchanan was saying. "Just that he called in and said he was unable to show up to work for the next several days."

"Right in the middle of filming?" Wright asked.

"Yes."

"Won't that be expensive?"

"The costs will be horrific. But Michael Steel is the consummate professional. I'm sure it must be something very, very important to him."

The image on the screen cut to Buchanan's and my argument Saturday night. I was taking Charlie's hand and storming toward the limousine as Wright resumed her report off camera. "And finally there is Steel's unusual interest in the still-unidentified minor ... and, of course, this all too revealing footage ..."

The picture cut to Cassandra racing from my house to her car, half naked, shouting, *"If you don't want to be with a woman, that's your business, Michael. But—little boys?"*

And then:

"You're sick, Michael! What you're doing is sick and disgusting and illegal and ... and sick! And you need help!" She slammed the car door and her tires squealed as she raced toward the gate. The image cut to a shaky zoom of Charlie approaching me in the driveway, reaching up to take my hand, wearing only his undershorts.

It was the first time I'd seen the footage and I felt numb and cold. But there was more. Now Mandy Wright stood outside my gate in the late afternoon sun—along with a fresh mob of reporters.

"So, in summary, what we have is an extreme interest in a little boy by Academy Award nominee Michael Steel ... clear accusations by his peers of sexual misconduct ... accompanied by his sudden and unexplained disappearance ..."

The image cut to a digitally enhanced replay of Charlie taking my hand as Wright continued, " ... all this coupled with the little boy's own disappearance from protective custody this morning and, well, one can only speculate whether there has been even more impropriety and foul play; whether perhaps the child has been abducted by Mr. Steel himself, in the continual unfolding of this strange and very bizarre—"

Annie snapped off the set. She'd seen enough. So had I.

I leaned against her desk, barely conscious of rubbing the rash on my arms. "Charlie's gone?" I asked.

Annie nodded. "I phoned. He's either run away or been abducted. Hasn't been seen since nine this morning."

"And they think I took him?" I asked incredulously.

"It doesn't matter what they think, Michael. The point is, we know the truth."

"That may work in the real world," I said, "but in mine, rumor and innuendo are nine-tenths of the law." I resumed scratching.

"I want to help you, Mikey, but I can't endanger the ministry. If they find out you're here, this whole place could—"

"No one has to know he's here."

We both turned to Big Bald who had remained in the doorway. He shrugged. "Us three, we're the only ones who know who you really are."

"You don't think the other residents have recognized—"

He shook his head. "They haven't said anything to me."

"Or me," Annie agreed.

"Too busy with their own issues to recognize something as inconsequential as a movie star—especially with his face all ugly and swollen." He shrugged. "No offense, Mr. Steel."

I nodded just as my cell phone chirped. I pulled it from my pocket and checked the incoming number. It was Kenny. I flipped it open and answered, "Hey."

"You see the news?"

"I just saw *Entertainment Today*. What are we going to do?"

"Do?" he sounded surprised. "Nothing. We're not going to do a thing."

"Are you crazy?" I started rubbing the rash on my neck. "Don't you hear what they're accusing me of?"

"Of course. It's perfect."

"Perfect?"

"A publicist's dream come true! Wire services all over the world are picking this thing up. You're becoming a household name!"

"Being branded a sexual pervert isn't exactly the publicity I was hoping—"

"No. Listen, this is perfect."

I threw Annie a look. She scowled at me rubbing my neck and I pulled my hand away.

Kenny continued. "We kick back a day or two, let the media heat this thing up until it reaches critical mass. And when they finally have enough rope to hang themselves, *bingo*—you emerge. Everything gets cleared up and you, my friend, become the innocent hero of a corporate smear campaign. I'm telling you, this is perfect. Judo to the max. The Art of War! Take the enemy's energy, turn it against him, and wind up everybody's hero. Even more so because you endured the attacks with silence and dignity!"

"Kenny—"

"I'm serious. Just don't go picking up any more stray boys and it's Hollywood legend time. I've already got a call in to one of the networks. Haven't told them the details but promised an exclusive when you decide to come out of hiding."

"*Hiding?*"

"It's just a term. They're already putting together footage. We're talking an hour special, Michael. On *you!* If we play this thing right—"

"Kenny!"

"—it could be the hottest entertainment story of the year. The decade! You think you were loved before, just wait until—"

"Kenny, I'm not interested."

There was a moment of silence. Then, "You're kidding, right?"

"I don't think so. I'm just not sure that—"

"You're not seeing the big picture."

"Maybe I'm not, I don't know, but—"

"Well I do. This is darkest-before-the-dawn time, amigo. All we need to—"

"Look." My head was pounding, I resumed rubbing my neck. "Give me some time on this, will you? I need time to think."

"Exactly. Take all the time you want. The longer the better."

"What about the Awards? The Academy vote?"

"Tomorrow's the last day. Whatever damage is done is done."

I took a deep breath and let it out.

"Don't sweat it, pal. Most of the votes are already in. And even if we lose, God forbid, there's always next year and the year after that and, well, you get the picture. You're about to become a legend, Michael! This is a gold mine handed to us on a silver platter!"

"Have you heard anything about Charlie?" I asked.

"The kid? Nothing. And that's good, too—the longer the better."

"But he could be hurt, he could—"

"Michael, the authorities will take care of him. He's not our concern. You and I, we've got bigger fish to fry."

One of the keys to Kenny's success is his understanding that "no" is simply the beginning of negotiation. It made little difference that I told him I was reluctant and undecided. To him, that was the same as "yes." And, to be truthful, nothing he said was really wrong. In many ways it made perfect sense. Let the media do all the work, generate all the publicity, then flip it around and emerge as the injured-yet-gracious victim.

It was an opportunity made in heaven . . . or hell.

— — —

"What do you think you're doing?"

I looked over my shoulder to see Annie's blonde assistant standing with her hands on her size one waist. It was 7:06 a.m. the following day, and after some major kitchen foraging I'd finally found the cereal bowls. "I was just grabbing some breakfast," I said, trying to sound as pleasant as possible—not an easy job with less than three hours' sleep under my belt. Despite the medicine and ointments, my itching and crawling skin made it impossible to think about anything at night . . . except my itching and crawling skin.

"If I were cold cereal," I asked, "where would I hide?"

"Breakfast was thirty minutes ago."

"Right. But—"

"This is no boarding house. You snooze you lose. Lunch is at 11:45."

"Actually, uh—"

"What detail are you on?"

"Pardon me?"

"Yard, attic cleanup, bathrooms, windows—what detail?"

I paused, taking a breath for patience. I can't tell you how badly I wanted to pull rank on this wannabe Gestapo. But after the last discussion with Annie about my prejudices, I was suspect of any feelings of superiority. So, instead of pointing out that I really wasn't a citizen of her little fiefdom, I played along.

"All right," I forced a grin. "How 'bout pointing me toward the coffee, then?"

"We don't have coffee."

"I'm sorry?"

"This is a drug-free environment."

Twenty minutes later I found myself in borrowed work clothes atop a ladder washing windows with a couple "bros" in the hot morning sun. My stomach growled for lack of food, my head pounded for lack of caffeine . . . and my ego whimpered from lack of respect. But I would not give in. I would be these people's equal if it killed me. By 11:15 we'd worked our way around to the outside of Annie's second-story office. If I feared (or hoped for) favored treatment, she put my mind to rest. She smiled, nodded, and returned to work—but not before pointing out a spot I'd missed.

I tried my best to fit in, pretending to enjoy the guys' street banter; their sexual vulgarities; their dissing of me for looking like a fat-faced version of that movie star—"What's-his-name"—they couldn't remember. Then, of course, there was my full-body rash leading to my new street handle: Leper Man. But the more trash they talked, the more they jived and bantered, the more I realized I would never fit in. I would always see myself as their superior. Who wouldn't? The best I could do was act like it was some part in one of my movies. Act like I thought we were equals, like I wasn't judging. But inside? Inside, I was just your typical, white-collar, politically correct . . . hypocrite.

The hours dragged into one day and then a second as we devoured meals of bread and spaghetti, bread and macaroni, bread and rigatoni (always with some token overcooked vegetable on the side). My 550-calorie-a-meal trainer would not be pleased. And, instead of getting better, I sadly saw myself growing worse. It seemed the more time I spent with the residents, the more I wanted to distance myself from them—recoiling at their ignorance, their simplemindedness, their reveling in the good old drug days and street life. And, as ashamed as I am to admit it, there were times, if we had too much physical contact, that I actually wanted to wash and shower to clean myself. No. I would never be like my sister. I would never love these people as myself. Black, brown, white—I was no racist, but an equal-opportunity bigot—I would never love them as Annie loved them.

Of course, I'd given a lot of thought to what she'd said about Christ's being the tree and our being the branches. I understood that it was our relationship with Him that empowered us. In a sense I suppose that's what had happened to me during Cassandra's and my little R-rated scene in the entry hall. But that had been a one-time occasion. How was it possible to practice this connection all the time? It wasn't. Like so much of the Bible, it made excellent theory, wonderful head knowledge. But it was one thing to understand His Word in my head . . . quite another for it to take root in my heart.

By the third day, my rash had started to disappear and I was finally getting some sleep. I had suggested going back to work, but Kenny said Robert Meisner and Colin Buchanan had already rescheduled. Besides, things were really getting interesting on the PR front, with sightings of Charlie and me in New York, San Francisco, London, and Amsterdam. Still, by Friday, I insisted that enough was enough and he finally agreed. It was time for me to "come out" and put an end to the rumors. Time to emerge as the mistreated hero.

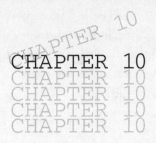

CHAPTER 10

The limo picked me up just south of Jeremiah's Place on Hollywood Boulevard. No good-byes to the residents, no heartfelt tears—just a prayer and kiss from Annie, followed by my silent departure.

We'd agreed to do the taping over at Burbank, where Kenneth met me in Makeup with fresh clothes and a boyish excitement I hadn't seen in years. Once I settled in, he left for some last-minute meetings with the producers. Our segment was to be taped midmorning. It would be edited with existing material and aired as a ten o'clock special that evening. The interview was to be friendly and casual, no hostile questions. Honesty and candor would be the tone, but a tone they'd let me set. I'd asked for one of the network's morning hosts, but they were booked, with no time to fly out from New York. Instead, we were assured that whoever they chose would be a sympathetic and seasoned pro.

As I sat in the old-fashioned barber chair, the makeup artist was polite but restrained. In her mind, the jury had already heard the evidence and reached their verdict. Fortunately, the TV up in the corner rattled away, filling our uneasy gaps of silence. Unfortunately, it was tuned to my old buddy, the televangelist, who had picked up right where he'd left off:

> *"Do not give dawgs what is sacred; do not throw your pearls to pigs.*
> *If you do, they may trample them under their feet, and then turn*
> *and tear you to pieces."*

I wasn't entirely sure what he was talking about. And I was grateful when we switched channels to some starving African kid, complete with flies and extended belly. The scenery wasn't any better, but the dialogue was. However, it did feel strange to be discussing which shade of $115-a-jar foundation to use or explaining how my hair had to be parted and waved just so, as the program's host pleaded for 50 cents a day to feed some kid.

Ironic? Yes.

Convicting? Of course.

Which was another reason I had decided to come clean. I was determined to put aside any pretense and tell the audience exactly what had been happening—how I'd been challenged by the teachings of Christ, how much of what occurred was the result of my trying to live those teachings, and how I'd failed time and time again.

That was my intention. Unfortunately, I should have given more heads up to what my preacher pal had just read.

– – –

"So you're saying this is all a result of God supernaturally messing with your life?" There was no missing the irony in my young interviewer's voice. Though I'd only seen her on the air once or twice, Network had assured us that Julie Reynolds was an up-and-coming Diane Sawyer. Young, candid, sensitive. Unfortunately, they'd left out another word . . . *ambitious.*

I cleared my throat, trying to soften her approach. "I don't know if '*messing with*' is the right phrase. But, yes, I definitely feel He's working in my life to teach me some valuable lessons."

"How thoughtful."

I wasn't sure how to respond. She saved me the effort. Shaking back her thick, red hair, she continued. "So, you'd say all these mix-ups—your strange behavior, your 'attraction' to this young boy, and his sudden disappearance, along with your own—"

"Look." Again I tried to diffuse the attack. "I know it sounds a little unusual, but if you'd just take a moment to—"

"A *little* unusual, Mr. Steel? A *little unusual?*"

"All right," I forced a chuckle, "a lot unusual." I could feel the rash on my neck starting to prickle and itch—no doubt from the additional blood running to my face.

"And," she continued, "more than just a little self-serving."

I threw a look at Kenneth who stood by one of the cameras. This was supposed to be a "friendly" interview; that was the agreement. But apparently nailing a hotshot on prime time was too good for the young opportunist to pass up. All right, if she wanted to play rough, I could play rough.

Immediately sobering, I said, "Listen, you asked me what was going on and I'm trying to tell you. But, if you continue to allow your own bias to—"

"You're trying to convince us that this is all some . . . 'Act of God.' That you, Michael T. Steel, take no responsibility for what's—"

"No, that's just it. I *am* taking responsibility."

"For sexually abusing a little—"

"Hold it!" I cut her off. "There was no sexual abuse. I've made that clear. There was no sex of any kind."

"So it would appear," she half-smirked. "As poor Cassandra, who threw herself at you during the night in question, and whom you sent running out of your house barely clothed, can attest."

I struggled for higher ground, keeping my voice even. "Cassandra is going through some very tough times right now."

"Is she."

"Yes. In our business, in our *cutthroat* business, when someone of her beauty and reputation reaches a certain age, they begin to . . . that is to say, they start losing their . . . what I mean is . . ." I came to a stop realizing there was no way to complete the thought without humiliating my friend and coworker in front of sixty million viewers. I cleared my throat. "Look, uh, can we stop tape and do that again?"

"Why's that, Mr. Steel?"

I stared at her. "'Why's that?' Because we've just damaged a good woman's career, that's why."

"Not *we*, Mr. Steel. It seems to me you're doing that all by yourself."

My face grew hotter. There was no reasoning with this one. I turned, shielding my eyes from the lights, looking off camera for the producer. "Can we stop tape and do that again, please?" But when I finally spotted him, he was not looking at me. Instead, he pretended to be in deep conversation with the floor director.

"Excuse me," I repeated.

The cameras continued to roll.

"Excuse me!"

I turned to Kenneth who appeared as alarmed at the double cross as I.

"So tell me, Mr. Steel," the reporter resumed, "is this another one of those little acts of God?"

I'd had enough. "Listen," I fought to keep my rage in check. "I don't know what you're trying to do, but there's no way I'm going to sit back and let you ruin—"

"I'm only looking for the facts, Mr. Steel. Facts that seem to be clearly speaking for themsel—"

"Facts?" That was it. I lost it. "*Facts?* You don't know the first thing about facts!"

"Is that so."

"Yes, that's so. You're not interested in facts. You're like the rest of us. All you care about is your career, about fighting and clawing your way up the food chain!"

She blinked, pretending to be unfazed. But I wasn't done.

"Well, don't fool yourself, Ms. Reynolds. You're nothing more than entertainment. Some circus clown in a power suit entertaining the masses."

"I see . . . and if I'm a clown, what does that make you, Mr. Steel?"

I reached for my lapel mic. Enough was enough. We'd been double-crossed, destroyed a colleague's reputation, and had now resorted to name calling. The interview was over. I unclipped the mic and rose from the chair.

"Are you leaving us, Mr. Steel?"

I didn't bother to answer. I spotted the producer who was urgently motioning to one of the cameramen to unlock his camera and go mobile.

"Mr. Steel—" Reynolds was also rising.

I dropped my mic to the chair and started off the riser.

"Mr. Steel!"

The cameraman scrambled to catch me.

"What about the child molestation, Mr. Steel? And assaulting reporters outside your house with poison oak? And what about this—"

The cameraman circled directly in my path.

"—little boy, this Charlie, supposedly lost in the system. Do you find these facts 'entertainment' as well?"

I moved to the left. Accidentally or intentionally, the cameraman moved the same direction, blocking me. I tried passing to his right, just as he also stepped to the right.

Reynolds continued dogging me from behind as I moved to the left again, and was blocked again. That's when I swore, cussing at him, shoving him out of my way. It was a stupid thing to do, but I was trapped and badgered and outraged. He stumbled backwards but didn't fall as I stepped down onto the black concrete floor and headed for the exit.

"Is this more evidence of God's work, Mr. Steel? Of your deeper commitment to Him?"

I was tempted to spin around and shout something back, but I'd already caused enough damage.

"Mr. Steel!"

I arrived at the exit, pushed open the heavy, soundproof door, and continued down the hall toward the lobby.

"Michael!" It was Kenneth shouting from behind. "Michael!"

But I wasn't stopping. Not for anybody.

"Michael!"

I stormed into the lobby with its life-size photos of TV and movie stars glowing in track lights. People froze, their eyes shooting to me. But I didn't care. I reached the glass doors, shoved them open, and stepped into the blinding sunlight.

– – –

The limo ride lasted forever as my thoughts churned and stormed. In that brief interview was there one command of Christ's that I had NOT broken? I doubt it:

Peacemaker . . . *Check.*

Merciful . . . *Check.*

Pure in heart . . . *Check.*

Meek . . . *Check.*

Somehow I'd managed to hit them all.

Persecuted for righteousness? Too bad there was nothing about being persecuted for stupidity . . . *Check.*

And salt and light? Call me a pessimist, but cussing someone out on national TV probably wasn't the best example of Christian behavior.

I glanced up and quickly called to the driver, "Here it is! Stop here!"

He hit the brakes. Before we even stopped, I threw open the door and climbed out.

"Mr. Steel," the driver shouted as I started up the hill into Annie's and my park. "Mr. Steel, should I wait here?"

"Yes . . . no . . . I don't care!"

I arrived at the peninsula of shrubs and trees, then followed them around until I came to the overgrown patch. I pushed my way through the oleander branches, one or two slapping me in the face, burning and stinging my eyes. But I didn't care. My eyes were already burning and stinging.

I continued down my mental checklist, bemoaning each of my failures. But it wasn't just self-criticism, not even my usual self-pity. Not this time. This time it was a cold, hard, undeniable fact. Not only had I failed in every area of my private life, I had also failed publicly— humiliating both myself and my God.

"I'm sorry!" I whispered hoarsely, "I'm so sorry . . ."

Of course there was no answer. Nothing except another branch to the eye.

I broke through the undergrowth and came to the clearing—panting for breath.

Directly in front of me stood Annie's tree.

I wiped my face, the sweat and tears stinging the welts. How could I travel so far to end right back where I started? Just a week ago I'd been sitting in the car outside Annie's place, aching over how defeated I was. I gave a scoffing laugh. *Defeated?* Compared to now, I hadn't known the first thing about the word. And yet, what had Annie said? That defeated was a good place to be—that it meant my hands were open and outstretched?

Well, she couldn't have been more wrong. My hands had been outstretched all week, begging, pleading, cajoling for help. But it made no difference. God had made impossible demands and He had given no hint on how to obey them. On the contrary, He'd actually allowed me to fail even more miserably.

Through clenched teeth I whispered, "What do You want from me?"

No answer.

I stepped closer to the tree. *"What?"*

Silence.

I was starting to tremble. Not in fear or weakness. But rage. Bubbling, roiling rage. "WHAT DO YOU WANT FROM ME?" I shouted. "WHAT MORE DO YOU WANT?"

Nothing.

"I BELIEVE IN YOU!"

"So do the demons, Toad." Annie's words went down no better now than when I'd first heard them.

"I've sacrificed everything!" I seethed. "Everything, and still I fail! And still I break Your commands!"

"It's not about breaking His commands, it's about breaking His heart."

"WHAT DOES THAT MEAN?"

There was no answer. The tears flowed faster. I swiped at them angrily. But they kept coming. I closed my eyes, then reopened them. The tree wavered in the moisture. So did the branches . . . and the little green buds that would soon become fruit.

" . . . *apart from me you can do nothing."*

But how could I do that? How could I become a part of Him? I *believed* in Him. I believed in Him just as surely as I believed in gravity. I believed in Him, but I was not *part* of Him. I worshiped. I obeyed. But I was not connected. Not really. And according to Annie, *according to Christ,* that's where the fruit came . . . from the connection.

"Just stay connected," she had said. *"Just fall in love with God and He'll do the rest."*

But *how?* I couldn't even do *that*. I took a ragged breath. How do you get connected to someone you've obeyed your whole life but haven't known?

My chest started to heave. I fought to swallow back a sob, but it escaped. And then another. Deep, jagged. The helpless sobs of a child.

"Please ..." I shoved my fist into my mouth, whispering fiercely. "Help me!"

There was still no answer.

Slowly, unconsciously, I sank to my knees. "Please ... please ..."

I lowered my head to the grass, hunched over. Helpless, sobbing, the veins in my face ready to explode. Yet even now I was unable to connect with Him, with the God I claimed to know.

And there I remained. Broken. Crying like a baby.

I had reached exhaustion. I rolled onto my side, still curled into a little ball. And there I lay, completely spent. How long did I stay like that? I don't know. But there was never an answer. Nothing.

Finally, I stirred. I raised my head toward the tree.

It remained as staunch and silent as ever.

Slowly I struggled back to my knees. Then, with some effort, rose to my feet.

Had I experienced any great revelation? Not a thing. Nothing but emptiness. An emptiness that came from being poured out. But that wasn't entirely bad. Because with that "pouring out" came a release of any expectation. And with that release ... freedom. There was no longer any self-criticism, no longer any self-loathing or self-pity. For the time being I was actually free of myself. It was the freedom of being completely empty, the freedom of being a total failure.

And yet ... a total failure who knew he was loved ... regardless of his failures.

Yes, it would have been nice to see a burning bush or to have the sky split apart with the shout of angels. I would have even settled for a "still small voice." But what I heard and saw and felt was ... nothing.

Nothing, except the knowledge that I had totally emptied myself before my Creator and had asked for His help. Nothing, except the knowledge that I couldn't even connect to His love without His help.

Some way, I don't even remember how, I made it back to the limo. Wasted and spent, I climbed into the backseat and mumbled something about heading for home. I didn't even notice the TV playing until we were headed down the road. On it was—what else, but preacher boy. I could only shake my head in amazement. But I didn't turn it off. I didn't have the strength. Instead, I leaned back into the seat and listened. Listened and realized that God was indeed answering my prayer. In this overweight, double-chinned, polyester-suit-of-a-man, God was already giving me His answer.

"Ask and it will be given to you; seek and you will find; knock and the door will be opened to you. For everyone who asks receives; he who seeks finds; and to him who knocks, the door will be opened. "Which of you, if his son asks for bread, will give him a stone? Or if he asks for a fish, will give him a snake? If you, then, though you are e-vil, know how to give good gifts to your children, how much more will your Father in heaven give good gifts to those who ask him!"

I wasn't asking for bread or fish. I was asking for something far greater. And I knew. From that moment on, I knew that I was now empty enough to receive it.

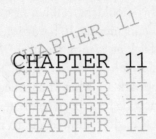

CHAPTER 11

Kenny's young assistant called from across my living room. "What time is the facial?"

"12:30," an even younger kid shouted.

"Hair?"

"11:15."

"Hair before the facial? Are you crazy!"

At last count, Kenneth had four of his people here at the house. Two just to manage phones. And for good reason. We were eight hours and counting to the Academy Awards. I had no way of comparing the surrounding craziness to what other nominees were facing—though I suspected Friday night's broadcast of my unedited interview added a bit more spice to the mix. Not that it mattered much. At least to me. Not like before.

"Mr. Steel, your wife's on line two."

I looked up from my three-by-five index cards.

"Tell her to be here by 4:30," Kenneth called.

"She wants to talk to Mr. Steel."

"He's not in."

"Kenny—," I protested.

"You don't need any more distractions," he said, taking my arm and leading me toward the French doors.

"I'm not going to lie to her," I said as he opened a door and pushed me onto the sundeck.

"Are you outside?"

"Yes, but—"

He shouted over his shoulder, "Tell her he's out!"

I shook my head, sadly musing. In a way it felt good to be back in the flurry of things, back at "Storm Central." Maybe *good* isn't the right word. Maybe it just felt ... more normal. Not that I'd forgotten what I'd learned in the park. Or what I had asked. But it was that asking, the freedom of knowing I was open to whatever God wanted, that gave me a certain peace, that allowed me to relax a bit these last couple of days.

"And his tanning appointment?" the assistant shouted.

"Everyone's booked," the underling cried.

"Booked!"

"There are no tanning bed appointments in a fifty-mile radius."

"Then buy one!"

Instead of running around trying to do good, I simply spent more time with Him. With *Him.* Not His rules, not His commands, but *Him.* As Annie had suggested, instead of looking for the fruit, I began looking at my Lord. And the more I looked at Him, the more I was beginning to sense a connection. I wasn't falling in love as she had promised, not yet. But something was happening.

"Where will I find a tanning bed in six hours?"

"Where will you find a job if you don't?"

"How's the speech coming?" Kenneth asked from the open door.

I glanced down at my index cards. "It's all right," I shrugged. "Not that I'll be needing it."

"Stranger things have happened, kiddo." Then under his breath he added, "Though I can't tell you when."

"It's Transportation, Line 1," the second assistant shouted. "They want Michael's limo to follow Gwyneth Paltrow."

"Follow?" Kenneth roared. "Michael Steel doesn't follow!"

"That's what they want."

"Tell them we're before Paltrow, or we're not at all!" Turning to me, he winked. "That'll get their hearts pumping." Spotting my Bible on the chair next to the door, he scooped it up and shoved it out to me. "Here, stay out of the way and make yourself useful." Then, just before shutting the door, he added, "And remind Him of the great PR He'll get if you win."

I smiled as the door closed. I stood there a moment, looking back through the glass, watching the people scurry back and forth in my little world. A world that I still enjoyed, but one I was feeling less and less attached to.

Kenneth was right; he had the machine up and running smoothly. There was nothing I could do now but stay out of the way . . . and pray. I turned and stared out over the water. Late morning fog still surrounded us, diffusing light and dampening sounds. Just beyond the surf, a lone pelican skimmed the swelling waves. I took a deep breath, smelling the fresh salty dampness. Then I headed to a deck chair near the railing, sat down, and flipped the Bible open to more of the Sermon:

> *"So in everything, do to others what you would have them do to you, for this sums up the Law and the Prophets."*

Ah, yes, the summary.

In many ways this was a condensation of all that I'd been reading. And yet I'd heard that in Christ's day the idea was mind-boggling. Before He came along, the creed had always been, *"Don't do to others what you don't want done to you"*—a fairly easy approach for most of us to follow.

Then came Jesus, flipping the statement on its head, suddenly making everything open-ended. Let's face it, just about anyone can succeed in *"not* doing to others what they *don't* want done to themselves." But *"doing* to others what you *want* done"—that can be never-ending. Like so many of His other commands, it calls for an impossible love that is impossible to accomplish.

I smiled to myself. Impossible to accomplish . . . *on my own.*

I looked back and continued reading.

> *"Enter through the narrow gate. For wide is the gate and broad is the road that leads to destruction, and many enter through it. But small is the gate and narrow the road that leads to life, and only a few find it."*

The *"narrow gate,"* that was the key. It wasn't so much in the doing as it was in the entering. Not in the racing around trying to fulfill commands but in the peaceful walking through the Gate, through that single Person. And once I'm connected to that Person, then the living He called me to do should happen naturally, instinctively . . . organically.

I took another breath and let it out. I hoped I had it right.

A moment later, the door opened and Kenny stepped out, offering me the phone. "It's Colin Buchanan," he grinned. "Wants to wish you luck."

I frowned, a little taken aback. "Why?"

Kenneth shrugged. "Probably figures there's a chance you might win."

It was my turn to smile. Though part of me wanted to decline the call, another part was reaching out and taking the phone naturally, instinctively, . . . organically.

– – –

"Watch out for false prophets. They come to you in sheep's clothing, but inwardly they are fee-rocious wolves."

"Do we have to listen to *him?*" Tanya complained.

I glanced up from the limo's TV screen. "Does it bother you?"

She shrugged. "Seems kinda weird, that's all. I mean, tonight of all nights."

She had a point. It *was* weird having the two worlds together. Especially tonight. Especially after all that I'd been through. It was like mixing oil and water; you can shake them all you want and for the moment they appear blended. For the moment. But eventually they separate. There was a good reason I had been feeling so schizophrenic. I *was* schizophrenic. I really had been trying to succeed in two separate worlds at the same time . . . and failing miserably in both. What had Annie said earlier? *"You're caught between two worlds, and it's tearing you apart."*

I nodded to Tanya. "You're right, he is irritating. It's just . . . I don't know, it's like we have this bond between us."

Tanya gave me a look.

I chuckled. "Believe it or not, he kinda gives me comfort. At least I know he's giving it to me straight up, without patronizing."

"Whatever," she sighed. She looked out at the passing ocean cliffs. "It's your night."

I smiled at her gently. "Is that why you wanted so badly to come, because it's *my* night?"

She turned to me.

I reached out and took her hand. "No, Tanya, it's *our* night. You worked as long and hard for this as I did."

She looked at me a moment, then turned back to the window and quietly removed her hand. It was a small gesture, but it felt as if she'd punched me in the gut. Odd as it seems, it was that moment, above all the others—above our drifting apart, above her moving out, even above the divorce papers—that told me it really was over. We could no longer fake it. The façade of the All-American Hero and his All-American Marriage was finally over.

"By their fruit you will recognize them. Do people pick grapes from thornbushes, or figs from thistles? Likewise every good tree bears good fruit, but a bad tree bears bad fruit. A good tree cannot bear bad fruit, and a bad tree cannot bear good fruit. Every tree that does not bear good fruit is cut down and thrown into the fire. Thus, by their fruit you will recognize them."

I swallowed the ache in my throat. It was so clear now. No make-believe relationship can last. Whether between husband and wife . . . or man and God. The real colors will eventually show. Sure, we can fake it, maybe for years, maybe decades. But if the relationship isn't healthy, the fruit won't be.

There it was again . . . *fruit.*

Coming from . . . *relationship.*

I shook my head, marveling at the pattern, musing how everything seemed to gravitate to the same truth.

I turned back to the TV:

"Not everyone who says to me, 'Lord, Lord,' will enter the kingdom of heaven, but only he who does the will of my Father who is in

heaven. Many will say to me on that day, 'Lord, Lord, did we not pro-phe-sy in your name, and in your name drive out demons and perform many miracles?' Then I will tell them plainly, 'I never knew you. Away from me, you evildoers!'"

I sat, chewing on the thought, realizing again how it was the *connection* that saved. It wasn't my claim of being Christian. It wasn't even the great things I did for Him. It was the connection . . . and the fruit, the obedience, that came from that connection. I turned toward the window, thinking, as I looked at the setting sun beyond a beach parking lot.

And that's when I saw it. The body. Lying facedown.

"Stop!" I shouted. "Stop the car!"

"What?" the driver called.

"Pull over! Pull over!"

Instinctively, he obeyed.

"Michael," Tanya asked, "what are you—"

"There's somebody hurt back there. In the parking lot."

"Are you sure?"

"Yes . . . I just saw them."

"But the time," she glanced at her watch. "Can't we just call the police? They can be here in—"

"Yes," I said as the limo stopped and I threw open the door. "Call the police!"

"Michael—"

I stepped outside.

"Michael!"

I barely heard her over the passing traffic as I started walking, then running, shielding my eyes against the sun.

Kenneth's Mercedes pulled in behind us. "What's wrong?" he shouted past his assistant as she rolled down the window.

"There's somebody out there!" I yelled.

"What?"

"In the parking lot! Somebody's hurt!"

"Michael, we don't have the time to—"

"There's an injured person back there!"

"Then let's call the ... Michael!"

I continued running, losing Kenny's voice to the wind and traffic. I approached a waist-high cinderblock wall. Trying to keep my tuxedo clean, I scampered over it. The body lay twenty-five yards ahead, face-down on the asphalt. Small. Not moving. Perhaps not breathing.

"Hey!" I shouted, running toward it. "Are you all right?"

There was no answer.

I scanned the parking lot. There was only a handful of cars and no people.

"Hey!" I was close enough to see it was a child. "Are you okay?" At last I arrived. He was breathing. Good. I stooped, still conscious of the need to not get dirty, and reached out to touch him. "Hey ..." Gently I shook him. "Hey, are you okay?"

He stirred and moaned softly. There was dark wetness on the asphalt surrounding his head.

"What happened?" I asked, fighting back panic. "Are you—"

He groaned again and finally turned over.

It was Charlie, his face covered in sand and blood. A gash ran from his forehead all the way to his jaw. "Charlie!" I dropped to my knees, slipping my hand under his bleeding head. "Charlie!"

His eyes fluttered, then opened.

"Charlie—"

Suddenly, he recoiled in fear.

"Charlie, it's me, Michael ..."

He tried sliding away, fighting me off, but I hung on.

"It's me, Michael. Charlie, it's Michael!"

Kenneth approached, shouting. "What's going on?"

"It's Charlie!"

He arrived, knelt down, then swore softly.

Charlie continued to fight, but I held him, trying to calm him. "It's okay ... it's me. Charlie, it's Michael. It's Michael!"

Kenny reached for his phone.

"What are you doing?" I asked. "Who are you—"

"911."

"Santa Monica is just down the road," I argued. "We could get him to the hospital faster than any ambulance."

Kenny nodded, letting the phone ring, checking his watch.

With one hand already under Charlie's head, I slipped the other under his knees to lift him.

"Michael!"

I glanced at Kenny. He looked anything but excited.

"What?"

"We don't have the time!"

"What are you talking about? It's Charlie!"

He opened his mouth, then glanced away, not answering.

I finished rising to my feet as Charlie continued squirming and fighting. "It's okay, Charlie, it's me, it's okay." He kept thrashing, smearing blood on my shirt, my tux, an errant hand occasionally catching my face. But the sound of my voice seemed to help, at least a little.

"Michael!"

I turned and saw Kenneth's frustration.

"We can't wait!" I shouted. "Look at his face! We've got to get him to the hospital now!" I started carrying him toward the highway.

"Michael!!" I slowed at the urgency in his voice. "You can't be seen with him! Not again!"

I turned and stared.

"911 has me on hold. I'll wait here. You go on."

"That's insane!" I yelled. Without waiting for a reply, I turned and continued toward the car.

Kenneth scrambled to my side. "You have any idea what they'll do to you if you're seen with him again!? The press? The *police?*"

"We've got to get him to a hospital!"

"I know," he agreed. "I know."

"*Now!*"

"All right!" He searched frantically for another solution.

I glanced down at Charlie. "Hang on, buddy," I said. "We'll get you there. Just hang—"

"Okay!" Kenneth shouted. "I've got it! *I'll* take him to the hospital!"

"Ken—"

"No, listen. *I'll* take him to Santa Monica. *You* keep on going."

"Look at him." I nodded down at Charlie's frightened eyes. "He's scared to death, he needs to be with someone he trusts."

"They'll crucify you!"

I continued forward. Kenny grabbed my arm. "Michael, think for a moment!" He moved in front of me, forcing me to stop. "Put him in *my* car. *I'll* take him."

I tried moving around, but he continued to block me. "They'll have a field day if they see you two together! And you'll never make it to the Awards. Not if you have to stay and file a report."

He was starting to make sense.

"Let me take him." he repeated. "He won't know the difference. Let me put him in *my* car. *I'll* take him."

I looked down at Charlie. He was barely conscious. It's doubtful he would know who had him. I glanced over at the limo. Tanya stood outside, shading her eyes from the sun.

"Come on, Mikey," Kenneth pleaded. "You can 'hear' that he's in the hospital *after* the Awards. *Then*, if you have to, *then* you can visit him. *Later*. But not now, not like this."

"You'll take him?" I asked. "You'll make sure everything's all right?"

"Of course. I'll take care of everything."

I took a deep breath, thought a moment, then finally nodded. It was as good a plan as any.

Kenny sighed in relief and we resumed toward the cinderblock wall.

"What's going on?" Kenneth's assistant stood outside the Mercedes, shouting.

"We found Charlie!" I yelled.

Kenneth scrambled over the wall, then turned and reached for Charlie. I passed the boy to him. But, sensing the change, Charlie started to twist and squirm again, smearing Kenny's own tuxedo with blood.

"It's okay," I shouted. "Charlie, I'm right here."

But it did no good. He fought harder, obviously wanting *me* to hold him.

I crawled over the wall as Kenneth moved to his car, struggling to hang onto the fighting child. His assistant opened the rear door, then headed to the front seat where she knelt backwards to console the boy. I arrived as Kenneth worked to untangle the seat belt and strap him in.

"It's okay!" I called from behind Kenneth, "I'm right here, Charlie! I'm right here."

Unable to see me, Charlie continued to panic. I ran to the other side, opened the door, and slid beside him. "Charlie, it's okay. I'm right here, I'm right here."

He saw my face and relaxed some. There was still fear in his eyes, but with me beside him he sensed he was safe.

It was then I realized I couldn't leave him. Not like this. Not with strangers. But there was no way Kenneth would let me ride with him. Not under these circumstances. Not under any circumstances. No amount of arguing would work. So, as he shut the door and started around toward the front, I leaped out and threw open the driver's door.

"Get out!" I shouted to the assistant as I slipped behind the wheel and shut my door.

"What?"

"Get out! Ride in the limo!"

Startled by my outburst and intimidated by my rank, she stepped outside . . . just as Kenny reached my door. I hit the lock button and shouted at her, "Shut it! Shut the door!"

She hesitated.

"What are you doing!?" Kenny yelled at me through the glass. He tried the door handle, then banged on the window.

I dropped the car into gear. "Shut the door!" I angrily repeated to the assistant.

She finally obeyed.

"Michael!" More banging.

I turned to him and shouted. "Go to the Awards! Go with Tanya to the Awards!"

He swore and slammed the window again. I tromped on the accelerator, throwing rocks and sand from the wheels.

"*Michael!*"

I swerved into traffic, generating plenty of honking horns—and I'm sure more swearing—as I raced towards the hospital.

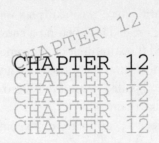

CHAPTER 12

CHAPTER 12
CHAPTER 12
CHAPTER 12
CHAPTER 12

Did I know I was endangering my career?

Yes.

Did I worry about it?

Yes. And no.

Yes, when I used common sense and realized what was happening. No, when I shoved reason out of my mind and thought with my heart.

Does that mean I believe God frowns on our using our minds and common sense?

Actually, I believe God uses common sense more than we think. He just works with a larger version of it than we give Him credit for. Isn't that what Peter did when he threw his feet over the side of the boat and walked on water—used Jesus' larger version of common sense? And that's what I was doing now. As Annie had suggested, I was throwing my feet over the side of the boat and, to my astonishment, found I was actually walking. As I raced into Emergency carrying Charlie against my bloodstained tuxedo, I was walking right over my smaller understanding of common sense. And, as long as I kept my eyes fixed on Jesus, I was able to do this impossible walking—naturally, instinctively, organically. As long as I kept my eyes fixed on His love, I was able to take the risk and love as *He* loved.

Did I panic? You bet. I panicked when staff members recognized me. I panicked when they asked me to fill out forms. I panicked when they discreetly picked up the phone and started making calls. But as long as I focused on my Lord and this needy child of His, I was able to do the impossible and walk as He walked.

The gash on Charlie's face was nearly six inches long. I asked to stay by his side as they rolled him behind a curtain, gave him a local painkiller, and started the stitching. He screamed and fought as they jammed the curved hook into his young flesh and pulled it out, then jammed it in again and pulled it out. He begged me with those huge, tear-filled eyes to make them stop.

"It's all right," I kept repeating, trying to comfort him and myself. "It's all right," I said as I helped hold him down. Because that's all I could do, comfort him and hold him. "It's all right, it's all right . . ."

Eventually the screams turned to pathetic whimpers. All the time those dark eyes remained locked onto mine . . . trying to believe in me, trying to trust me.

"I know," I said, wiping my own eyes. "It won't be long, I promise, it won't be long."

But it was long. Impossibly long. As the needle continued poking in and pulling out, poking in and pulling out.

Silent tears rolled down his cheeks, but he eventually stopped fighting and I was able to release him. Yet, when I rose, he grabbed my hand, squeezing it fiercely as the needle went in and came back out. I understood and let him hold it, feeling the pain myself, with each squeeze, with each poke and pull. Together, the two of us would get through this.

We were about halfway when I heard the TV from the waiting room come on. It was the opening of the Academy Awards. Was I curious? Of course. But there were more important things to do.

The needle continued, in and out, in and out, in and out—until finally, finally, the doctor looked up. He removed the magnifying glass, then his gloves, and sighed with a nod.

"We're done!" I cried. "Charlie, we're done!"

He looked up at me, his face flooding with relief.

I grinned. "And you, my little friend, are going to have one very sexy scar when you get older."

For the first time that evening, I saw a trace of his crooked-tooth grin. It wasn't much, but enough to swell my heart until it nearly burst.

"We'll have to keep him overnight," the doctor said.

"For observation," I added, as if I thought we were in consultation.

"And X-rays," he said.

"Yes, of course, X-rays."

They wheeled him into an adjacent hall where the two of us waited nearly forty-five minutes for a room to be prepared—me, making idle chitchat about my misadventures at Jeremiah's Place—and Charlie smiling, starting to relax. Between the torture he'd just come through and whatever trauma he'd recently suffered on the streets, the poor kid was past exhaustion. I watched as his eyes grew heavier and heavier. He fought to keep them open, but it was no use. Soon he'd fallen asleep. But I didn't remove my hand. Whenever the temptation rose to track down the distant TV and find out what was happening, all I had to do was look down at that face and see that hand clinging to mine. I knew I was right where I should be.

Eventually the room was ready and we rode up the elevator. Charlie awoke only when the doors rattled open, and then just for a moment. We rolled him out and I stayed glued to the side of his gurney as we headed down the hall. More than one pair of eyes recognized me. Some stared unabashedly at my bloodstained shirt and tuxedo. Others frowned when they saw I was holding his hand.

We had barely entered the room and transferred him to his bed when I heard: "Mr. Steel?"

I turned to see a Santa Monica policeman standing in the doorway.

"May I speak with you a moment?" he asked.

"Sure." I turned to Charlie who had heard the voice and tried unsuccessfully to open his eyes. I whispered, "Listen, Charlie, I uh, I have to talk to the officer for a couple—"

His fingers tightened their grip on my hand.

I turned to the officer. "Can you give us just a minute?"

He nodded.

I turned back to Charlie and whispered. "I'll be back, I promise."

His forehead creased into a frown.

"Hey, have I ever lied to you before?"

The scowl remained.

Suddenly I recalled the ID from the Chad Slayter spy car, the prop he'd been so captivated by a week earlier. I reached into my pocket and pulled it out. "Remember this?" I asked.

With effort, he opened his eyes a crack, then smiled.

"Well, I want you to do me a favor." I began removing the plastic "C. S." from my key ring. "I want you to hang on to this for a while, okay?"

His eyes opened further.

"I want you to keep it safe for me. Do you think you can do that?"

He stared at the initials, transfixed.

"Just for a little while, okay? Just until we get together again. All right?"

He tried to nod.

"You sure?"

Another half smile, then his eyes slowly closed.

"Good." I reached down and placed the initials in his free hand. "Here you go, then."

He gripped them, slowly turning them in his fingers, but not reopening his eyes.

"And when we get back together again, you'll give it to me, okay?"

A fainter smile as his fingers continued to work.

"Is that a deal, Charlie? Do we have a deal?"

The fingers gradually slowed.

"Charlie . . ."

Finally, they stopped altogether. I waited another moment, before gently pulling my hand from his. He offered no resistance. I felt the familiar tightness in my throat as I reached down and also placed his other hand on the initials. I hesitated a moment, then leaned over and gently kissed the small unbandaged part of his forehead. "Good night, Charlie," I whispered. "I'll see you a little later." I stood a moment, staring down.

"Mr. Steel?"

I turned to the officer.

"Would it be possible for you to come down to the station with me for some questions?"

"Do I have a choice?"

"Yes, sir. But I think it would be better for you if you came."

I searched his eyes and saw the sincerity. Slowly I nodded. The officer stepped back to the door to give me one last moment with Charlie. I looked at the boy as he lay sleeping soundly.

Finally I turned and joined the officer. We moved down the hall under the gaze of a half a dozen staff members. I waited until we were in the elevator and the doors closed before asking, "Do you think I should call my lawyer?"

"Yes, sir," he said, "I think that would be a very good idea."

We rode the rest of the way in silence. When the elevator came to a stop, the doors opened to the lobby. Not far away, through smudged glass, I saw two, maybe three news crews already assembling. The officer cursed quietly under his breath.

We moved across the room, and just before we reached the doors he asked, "You ready for this?"

"As ready as I'll ever be."

He nodded. We arrived and the doors hissed open.

"There he is!" a voice shouted. "He's here!"

Immediately, the lights glared on and the carnival began . . .

"Mr. Steel, where were you keeping the boy?"

"Michael, do you have any idea how your public will respond?"

The officer patiently directed me through them toward the car where his partner waited with the rear door already open.

"Michael, what will your defense be?"

"How will you plead?"

The second officer reached out and gently guided me toward the open door.

"How is the boy?"

"Mr. Steel, what does it feel like to win?"

I hesitated, then looked across the roof to the reporter, unsure what he meant. "Win?" I asked.

"Well, yes. Surely you know you've just won the Academy Award for Best Actor. How does it feel?"

I said nothing. What could be said? I do, however, remember smiling as the officer protected my head and eased me down into the seat before shutting the door. But, even then, as the cameras pressed to the window, as they recorded my smile, I knew it would be misunderstood. I knew to some it would be proof of a sick, out-of-control movie star who obviously cared more about winning an Oscar than about a little boy's welfare.

Of course, that was far from the truth. Yet, even as we pulled away, I kept on smiling. I couldn't help myself. I'd won, all right. But it had nothing to do with the Academy Award. It was a different type of winning altogether.

EPILOGUE

EPILOGUE
EPILOGUE
EPILOGUE
EPILOGUE

FADE IN:

INT. HEAVEN—DAY
The Accuser of the Brethren and his Creator are
having another debriefing.

>   GOD
>   Where have you come from?

>   SATAN
>   Please . . .

>   GOD
>   Where have you come from?

>   SATAN
>   [reluctantly quoting]
>   "From going to and fro in the earth,
>   and from walking up and down in it."

>   GOD
>   Have you considered my servant,
>   Michael?

>   SATAN
>   [wearily]
>   Yes.

>   GOD
>   Didn't think he'd come through, did you?

                    SATAN
Do I detect a bit of pride?

                    GOD
It's a Father's privilege.

                    SATAN
All right, so he found the key to
those Kingdom Principles of Yours.
What makes You think he'll keep on
living them?

                    GOD
He won't.

                    SATAN
He'll fail?

                    GOD
From time to time, they all do.

                    SATAN
And that doesn't bother You? Having a
kingdom of failures?

                    GOD
They're the only ones who win.

                    SATAN
I'm telling You, he'll fall again.

                    GOD
And when he does, he'll fall toward
Me.

                    SATAN
             [spotting something
                in God's hands)
What do You have there?

                    GOD
Oh, just a little memento.

                    SATAN
It's the initials! The key to Chad
Slayter's spy car!

                    GOD
Pretty, aren't they?

                   SATAN
What are You doing with them?

                    GOD
Charlie brought it back.

                   SATAN
Charlie! I thought your emissary was
that televangelist.

                    GOD
That's right.

                   SATAN
And Charlie, too? Don't You think
that's a little overkill?

                    GOD
I like to win.
          [admiring the key]
It's a touching souvenir, don't you
think?

                   SATAN
You can be so sentimental sometimes.

                    GOD
It's a Father's privilege.
       [Having had enough, Satan
        scoffs and turns to EXIT.]

                    GOD
Where're you going? What's the rush?

                   SATAN
Time's running out. I've got to find
some more.

                    GOD
Good idea. The more you bring Me, the
better.

                    SATAN
          [stopping in his tracks]
You?! Bring *You!?* I'm not doing this
for You! I'm doing it for me.

                    GOD
After all these millennia you still
buy that?

                    SATAN
I have no choice. To believe otherwise
would mean acknowledging You as . . .
as . . .

                    GOD
Sovereign Lord and King?

                    SATAN
          [turning to leave]
I have to go.

                    GOD
Have it your way.

                    SATAN
I wish I could . . .
          [muttering as he exits]
. . . just once, I wish I could.

                              FADE OUT

I thought back to that final dream of so many months ago while the
young seminary graduate, Daryl, continued explaining why he was
best qualified to fill Annie's position at Jeremiah's Place. He was
longer-winded than most, but when I sensed he was finally running
down, I looked up from Annie's desk and asked a single question.
"Why on earth would you want to work at a place like this?"

    "Why?" He looked startled. "*Why?* Well, because that's what God
commands us to do."

    "How so?"

    "*How so?*" He sounded equally startled.

                         -156-

I nodded.

He quoted, "'Go and make disciples of all nations.' That's a command."

"I appreciate that," I cleared my throat. "But tell me—"

"'Whatsoever you do for the least of these you do for me.' 'Sell everything you have and give to the poor, and you will have treasure in heaven.'"

"Yes, those are worthy aspirations—"

"They are not aspirations, Mr. Steel. They are commands."

"Yes . . . they are worthy *commands*. But the folks here," I nodded to Big Bald who sat beside him, "they put in some long and grueling hours. What makes you so sure you have the stamina?"

"You saw my transcripts?"

"Yes, your grades are very impressive."

"And my community service projects?"

"Yes, equally impressive. It's just . . . I guess my real question is, how well are you and God getting along?"

"Sir?"

"What's your relationship like with Him?"

He broke into an understanding smile. "Oh, that . . . Let's see, I've been attending church regularly since I was eight. I was president of my youth group the last two years of high school. I've been teaching Sunday school since I was a sophomore in college. And I've been volunteering as a youth pastor throughout seminary."

Big Bald whistled.

I agreed. "You're one busy guy."

"Thank you, sir."

I stared down at his application a long moment before looking up. "Listen, would you mind swinging by again, tomorrow? There's one more thing I need to show you."

"Certainly." He pulled out his Palm Pilot. "Morning or afternoon?"

"Is eight a.m. too early?"

"No, sir, I'm usually through my devotions by 7:15. In fact, we could make it earlier, if you like."

I cleared my throat. "No, eight will be fine."

"Eight it is."

As he entered his appointment, I stood up. He followed suit and we shook hands. "I really want to thank you for your consideration, Mr. Steel."

"You're certainly welcome. Eight o'clock, then."

He nodded, turned to shake Big Bald's hand, and walked out into the hallway, all of three steps. We said our final good-byes and, after he was gone, I quietly shut the door.

"So what do you think?" Big Bald asked as he sat back in his chair.

I paused, thinking.

"Sure sounds committed."

I nodded. "Yes, he does."

Stretching, Big Bald added, "'Bout as perfect as they come, if you ask me."

"Yeah," I continued to nod, "perfect. At least that's what he's trying to be, isn't it?"

"Which is why you're taking him to the park tomorrow?"

I looked up, surprised.

He broke into a grin. "Gonna visit Annie's tree?"

"You know about that?" I asked. "She showed you?"

"'Course she did." His grin broadened. "Why else you think I'm here?"

I returned the smile until it faded into quiet memories. "You miss her?" I asked.

"Like a piece of my heart is gone."

"Me too," I nodded. "Me too."

Heavy silence filled the room. Annie had been gone two months now. But not from the HIV she'd contracted. No, that would have been too predictable for my Annie. Instead, she'd been broadsided one November night by a drunk driver at an intersection just a few blocks from the house . . . as she drank her decaf tea.

It was a completely random act, totally senseless . . . at least by our standards. She died two days later from complications—but not before making it clear to her Board of Directors that Big Bald and I were the ones to choose her successor.

Why she wanted me, I hadn't a clue. But the board grudgingly agreed. *Grudgingly* because, although I'd been found innocent of all charges, my name and reputation still had a certain . . . how should I put it? . . . *stench*. A stench that did not improve when Charlie again disappeared, this time never to be found. A stench that sent my career into a tailspin. I had received a few mid- to low-level offers, but not one substantial film project had come my way in the last nine months. Apparently even an Academy Award doesn't help when it comes to sick, emotionally unstable pedophiles who cleverly kidnap and dispose of their victims. I may have been innocent in the eyes of the law, but the studios suspected that the ticket-buying public had reached a much different verdict.

"You know," Big Bald said, drawing me from my thoughts. "There might be somebody else better for this job, somebody so close that we've been overlooking them."

I turned to him and grinned. "You're reconsidering? You're finally thinking of taking the position?"

He shook his head. "Wasn't talking about me."

"Who then?"

He cocked his head and raised an eyebrow.

I blinked in surprise. "What? *Me?*"

"You certainly got the heart."

"I don't know the first thing about street life."

"Neither did Annie, 'til I came around."

I shook my head, chuckling. "Look, I appreciate the compliment, but I've got my career."

He cocked his head the other direction.

"Okay, I *had* my career."

He waited, letting the silence build.

"You're serious, aren't you?"

No answer.

I continued, incredulous. "You honestly believe I could do something like this?"

At last he spoke. "Not you, man." Taking another long stretch, he rose to his feet. "You couldn't even come close."

I frowned. "Then, what—"

"Not on your own, anyway. But you got yourself some great connections."

I shook my head. "My name mean's nothing now. I can't even get my agent to return my—"

"Not those connections, man. The other."

I looked on, still not understanding.

He threw a glance upwards, answering my question.

I smiled, finally getting it . . . but not buying it.

He continued. "That Daryl—the others—they know all there is to know about Him . . . but they don't *know* Him. Not like you."

I blinked again, somewhat startled.

He gave a chuckle. "Just give it some thought, man. *He'll* let you know." With that he turned and started for the door. "Just give it some thought."

"It would certainly be one for the books," I said as I headed back to the desk. "A real surprise."

"From what I've seen, the Dude is full of 'em."

I glanced up at him but Big Bald had already stepped into the hall and was lumbering out of sight.

Musing at the absurdity of the idea, I eased myself into Annie's chair. It was true. God was full of surprises, no doubt about it. But not this. Not me. I chuckled softly. Then, spotting Annie's Bible, I reached for it and flipped to the last section of the Sermon on the Mount. And there, in the quiet of the office, I started reading it, just as I had so many times during the last few months . . .

"Therefore everyone who hears these words of mine and puts them into practice is like a wise man who built his house on the rock. The rain came down, the streams rose, and the winds blew and beat against that house; yet it did not fall, because it had its foundation on the rock. But everyone who hears these words of mine and does not put them into practice is like a foolish man who built his house on sand. The rain came down, the streams rose, and the winds blew and beat against that house, and it fell with a great crash."

It's true, the rain had come down hard in my life, very hard. And the wind had blown. But by practicing His words, or at least trying to, I had somehow survived. Not only survived, but I suppose, in a strange sort of way, I had flourished.

I had flourished during that nightmarish week before the Academy Awards.

I had flourished watching my career go down the drain.

And I knew I would flourish wherever He put me, regardless of how silly or foolish it might appear. All I had to do was stay connected.

Stay connected, and leave the rest up to Him . . .

Bible Study Questions

Below are some thoughts from each chapter. Instead of downloading information, I've put them in the form of questions so they are a bit more interactive. As you think them through, be sure to ask the Holy Spirit for His insight.

Prologue/Chapter One

1. Why is it so important for the Satan character to choose someone like Michael?

2. In Luke 18:25 Jesus says, "Indeed, it is easier for a camel to go through the eye of a needle than for a rich man to enter the kingdom of God." Is that true for Christians, too? How does your answer apply to Christ's words to the Church in Laodicea, Revelation 3:14–22?

3. How are you hungry and thirsty?

4. How are you not?

5. What can be done to change that?

Chapter Two

1. Was Michael really blessed for being merciful, pure in heart, and a peacemaker?

2. How do you function in these capacities?

3. How are you hurt when you practice them?
4. How are you blessed?

Chapter Three

1. Michael struggles with tough questions regarding being persecuted for righteousness. How do we know when we're being persecuted for righteousness or when we're just looking to be a martyr?
2. What's the difference between being salt and being light?
3. Is it possible to be too much of either?
4. How can we know?

Chapter Four/Interlude

1. Jesus Christ said that He didn't come to abolish the Law and the Prophets but to fulfill them. How?
2. How is it possible for our righteousness to surpass that of the Pharisees and teachers of the Law?
3. In the story, God tells Satan the key to the dilemma was nearly discovered during Michael's kiss with Cassandra. How does God defeat Satan with Satan's own victories? Can you name situations in Scripture where God's greatest victories came from the darkest moments?
4. Can you name some in your own life?

Chapter Five

1. In Matthew 5:39 Jesus says, "Do not resist an evil person." What about the Hitlers of the world? Should Michael have let the press walk over him? Where did he step over the line in his actions? In his heart?
2. Earlier, in Matthew 5:16, Jesus says, "Let your light shine before men, that they may see your good deeds . . . ." But in this section

He warns us about not parading our righteousness before others. What's the difference in Michael's life? What's the difference in yours? (Hint: I've only quoted the first half of Matthew 5:16.)

3. Michael walks out of church because he feels he's a hypocrite. Was that true? Is there a difference between someone who tries and fails and someone who is a hypocrite? Who can tell that difference?

Chapter Six

1. This entire chapter covers the Lord's Prayer (though the prayer is worth an entire novel ... or two). Each portion is divided and covered in Michael's separate ruminations. If time permits, it would be great to dwell on each portion of the prayer for yourself (with or without a mountain bike).

2. Among other elements, forgiveness plays a substantial part in this prayer. There's a sobering parable on forgiveness in Matthew 18:21–35. Take a look at what God calls the unforgiving servant in verse 32. Is that fair? How is this man "wicked" if he is legitimately owed the money? How are we "wicked" if we don't forgive someone who legitimately hurts us?

3. Compare the end of this parable (verse 35) with the end of the Lord's Prayer section of Matthew 6:14–15. Why does God put such an emphasis on forgiveness?

Chapter Seven

1. The themes in this chapter revolve around heavenly riches and worldly wealth. Though we clearly see the difference, how are we seduced into pursuing the world's wealth?

2. How does fear play a factor in this seduction?

3. Interesting that Jesus ends this section of the Sermon by reminding us that God will take care of us. In what areas do you accept this? In what areas do you struggle with it? How can you succeed in believing it?

4. In my novel *Eli* (a retelling of the Gospel as if it were to happen today instead of 2000 years ago) and my children's fantasy, *The Bloodstone Chronicles*, reference is made to earth being an Upside-Down Kingdom (when compared to the Kingdom of God). In what ways other than wealth do we see and do things upside down from His Kingdom?

Chapter Eight

1. This chapter explains the theme of the book. It's restated during Jesus' farewell speech to the disciples in John 15:5–8, which is worth rereading. How have you seen this principle work in your own heart?

2. There's an old hymn that was later used in the musical, *Godspell*. It talks about praying each day to gradually see God better ... which leads to loving Him more deeply ... which leads to obeying Him more perfectly.

   How does that progression tie in with the theme? With our lives?

Chapter Nine

1. This chapter examines judging and prejudices. Christ states that as we judge, we'll be judged. Have you seen this principle at work here on earth?

2. Are we called to be naive to the evil and dangerous people around us?

3. In 1 Corinthians 5:9–13, Paul is very clear that we are not to associate with brothers who are sexually immoral, greedy, idolaters, slanderers, drunkards, or swindlers. How does this compare to Jesus' command to us not to judge?

4. A pastor friend once said we know we have the right spirit of love and humility if we see a brother sinning and *don't* want to confront him. What does he mean?

5. How do these insights fit into the theme of the book?

Chapter Ten

1. In what ways did Michael give what was holy to dogs? Have you ever made that mistake? How can we make the distinction without "judging"?

2. How is Michael's situation at the end of this chapter similar to Annie's first encouragement regarding his being hungry and thirsty?

Chapter Eleven

1. At this portion in the Sermon Jesus states, "Not everyone who says to me 'Lord, Lord,' will enter the kingdom of heaven." I often tell students that if they find something radical in Scripture, make sure they find it in at least two other locations to ensure they're not taking it out of context. How does this section compare to Christ's chilling parable of the sheep and the goats in Matthew 25:31–46? Or, again, in His promise to the church of Laodecia regarding their deeds in Revelation 3:15?

2. Does this cancel the many verses in the Bible which tell us we are saved by our "faith" in Jesus Christ?

3. How do our "works" serve as a thermometer to gauge our "faith"?

Chapter Twelve

1. Why was it important that Michael face this challenge in the story now and not earlier?

2. Why not later, after his victory at the Awards?

3. Why is it important that God test us? Doesn't He know what we'll do before we do it? How does James 1:2–4 apply to this?

Epilogue

1. In the story, God tells Satan that only those who fail will win. What does He mean?

2. If Michael chooses to stay, what will be his strengths? His weaknesses?

   How does this apply to what Paul wrote in 2 Corinthians 12:10, "For when I am weak, then I am strong," or to his promise in Romans 8:28?

3. In your own life, with your own calling, how can God use your strengths?

4. How can He use your weaknesses?

Once again, thanks for taking this journey with me. I hope you found it as interesting as I did.

What If You Could Hear the Voice of God?
What If You Actually Saw His Face?

The Face of God

BILL MYERS

That is the quest of two men with opposite
faiths . . .

THE PASTOR

His wife of twenty-three years has been murdered.
His faith in God is crumbling before his very eyes. Now, with his
estranged son, he sets out to find the supernatural stones spoken of
in the Bible. Stones that will enable the two of them to hear the audi-
ble voice of God. Stones that may rekindle their dying faith and love.

THE TERRORIST

He has also learned of the stones. He too must find them—but for
much darker reasons. As the mastermind of a deadly plot that will
soon kill millions, he has had a series of dreams that instruct him to
first find the stones. Everything else is in place. The wrath of Allah is
poised and ready to be unleashed. All that remains is for him to
obtain the stones.

With the lives of millions hanging in the balance, the opposing
faiths of these two men collide in an unforgettable showdown. *The
Face of God* is another thrilling and thought-provoking novel by a
master of the heart and suspense, Bill Myers.

Softcover: 0-310-22755-0
Adobe® Acrobat® eBook Reader: 0-310-25702-6
Microsoft® Reader: 0-310-25764-2
Palm™ Reader: 0-310-25705-0
Unabridged Audio Pages® CD: 0-310-24905-8
Unabridged Audio Pages® Cassette: 0-310-24904-X

Pick up a copy at your favorite bookstore!

Blood of Heaven
BILL MYERS

Mass Market: 0-310-25110-9
Softcover: 0-310-20119-5

Threshold
BILL MYERS

Mass Market: 0-310-25111-7
Softcover: 0-310-20120-9

Fire of Heaven
BILL MYERS

Mass Market: 0-310-25113-3
Softcover: 0-310-21738-5
Abridged Audio Pages® Cassette: 0-310-23002-0

Eli
BILL MYERS

Mass Market: 0-310-25114-1
Softcover: 0-310-21803-9
Abridged Audio Pages® Cassette: 0-310-23622-3
Palm Reader: 0-310-24754-3

When Everything Seems Lost, God's Love
Has a Way of Turning Life Around.

When the Last Leaf Falls
A Novella

BILL MYERS

This retelling of O. Henry's classic short story, *The Last Leaf,* begins with an adolescent girl, Ally, who is deathly ill and angry at God. Her grief stricken father, a pastor on the verge of losing his faith, narrates the story as it unfolds.

Ally's grandpa lives with the family and has become Ally's best friend. He is an artist who has attempted—but never been able—to capture in a painting the essences of God's love. One day, in stubborn despair, Ally declares that she will die when the last leaf falls from the tree outside her bedroom window. Her doctor fears that her negative attitude will hinder her recovery and her words will become a self-fulfilling prophecy.

This stirring story of anger and love, of doubt and hope, speaks about the pain of living in this world, and the reality of the Other world that is not easily seen but can be deeply felt. Talented storyteller Bill Myers enhances and updates a storyline from one of the masters and brings to light the awesome power of love and sacrifice.

Hardcover: 0-310-23091-8

We want to hear from you. Please send your comments about this book to us in care of zreview@zondervan.com. Thank you.

GRAND RAPIDS, MICHIGAN 49530 USA

WWW.ZONDERVAN.COM